Star-crossed Lovers

E.A. Harper

Chapter One

The pale moon rose against the dark night sky as a cool sea breeze drifted in along the shore of Doorus. The small fishing village edged into a corner of Galway Bay, which overlooked the vast North Atlantic Ocean in the west of Ireland. The Aran Islands stood out across the entrance of the bay amongst a cluster of smaller islands. This was an enchanted place where it often felt as though; the hands of time stood still anticipating the mystical forces of nature caressing the earth.

The sinking sun left a trail blaze of burnt orange, set against a sky streaked with pink clouds, which merged with inky blue on the distant horizon. The rocks above the shore line cast down dark foreboding shadows as their silhouette's lengthened. The warm haze of the long summer's day had finally given way to the cooler shades of evening time.

Elena sat alone on the deserted beach observing the sunset, and contemplating her life. She had been travelling around the coast of Ireland, camping at various sites along the way. She had seen many beautiful places during the last few months, but this one called to her soul. Furthermore her spirit felt restless as if assuming that something important was about to occur.

Elena possessed the rare gift of clairvoyance; she had discovered this at an early age. As a consequence she had grown up being drawn further into an occult, esoteric path of life. She willingly accepted her gift becoming an accomplished white witch. Through the years she had studied natural medicines and potions.

Learning all there is to know of this very ancient craft. Sadly this gift conjointly set her apart from others. She was considered a bit of a misfit in the regular rat race society of suburban England. She had very few friends or any real family, in which to relate to. Her life would have been a solitary existence if not for her companion, a scruffy mongrel dog called Pagan. Elena longed for a place somewhere although she knew not where, but a place where she could set her soul free, and maybe find love. She sat daydreaming about love, and what it would be like to fall madly in love as a lot of young women do. In her mind she created wild imaginings and fanciful notions. She imagined a handsome young man who would carry her away into the sunset. She closed her eyes momentarily sighing dreamily, but when she opened them again there were the old familiar surroundings, back to back houses, loud unkempt people, rubbish strewn streets and dark grey overcast skies.

So one day out of the blue Elena decided quite impulsively to just opt out. She explained her decision to her dog Pagan. He cocked his furry head to one side, and attempted to pay attention. He looked at her adoringly with his soft, velvety brown eyes. He would follow her to the ends of the earth; such was his loyalty, which is rarely matched by human souls.

By the end of the week she had cashed in her savings, and bought a camper van. She packed up her things consisting of mainly clothes, books, dried herbs, and a small wooden chest, which contained ointments and potions each neatly labeled. She locked up the house, and popped the key under a large stone at the edge of the flower bed. Elena left the neat little terraced house, which had been her home for many years without a backwards glance. She drove her camper van on through the evening heading for Anglesey, and the sea port of Holyhead. She felt determined and an air of excitement cursed through her body. She felt sure a great adventure lay before them. Elena reached over and patted Pagan's furry head; he sat upright next to her on the passenger seat, and licked her hand gently. She was pleased with the vans performance so far. For a second hand van it drove pretty smoothly, and despite it having clocked up 200,000 miles from its previous owner.

In a few hours they had reached Holyhead, which was a grey windswept port. There were a few other cars waiting in line at the bay to board the ferry. Elena parked up, and let Pagan out to stretch his legs. The wind was sharp, and the night air had a damp misty hue. The salty sea air carried water droplets inland. She checked her travel documents feeling a slight nervous moment as her ticket was only one way. Elena shrugged her shoulders; she decided to get hot chocolate and a sausage roll for Pagan from the nearby service station. Afterwards they sat in line eating as they waited to board. Eventually the time passed by, and soon enough they were traveling onboard the swift ferry at midnight towards Ireland. The crossing was bumpy and a few people were ill with travel sickness. Elena went up on top deck and hung on tightly to the guard rail. The wind blew her hair around her face in strong gusts and she found it difficult to catch her breath. The lights of the port faded away behind them as she surveyed the vast inky black swirling ocean. Her mind was calm and unperturbed, gone were the last minute nerves of doubt and uncertainty. She felt relief that she had at last escaped from the rat race.

A few hours on and they had crossed the Irish Sea as they arrived at Dublin port. It was still relatively dark but the sky was now merging from jet black into lighter tones of grey daubed with dark blue. Elena drove her van keeping in line with the queue of cars ahead. Eventually they disembarked from the huge ferry. Pagan slept soundly on the seat beside her as they arrived in Dublin city. It was brightly lit up and the pubs and bars were still open, full of late night revelers. She drove on past them following the road signs headed southwards as quickly as the traffic had allowed. Dublin, although lively and exciting, did not appeal in the slightest. Elena had already decided that they would escape from the city as fast as they could. She had a vision in her mind, of where destiny was taking them. She had seen a place vividly in her dreams, although the name of this place had not been revealed. Elena knew well that it would be far too easy, to be given all the pieces to the puzzle of life. She was meant to find this place by her own free will.

It was evening time; Elena gazed out across the dark ocean, watching the swaying motion of the waves. The deep waters swelled majestically as they heaved to and fro, pulled by the magnetic force of the moon. It was the middle of June and the weather was becoming increasingly warmer. She and Pagan had been traveling in Ireland for almost a month by now. They had followed the coastal roads, and had stayed at various campsites. As a consequence they had met some very friendly people along the way. Irish people seemed to have a natural calm, and casual nature. This was a refreshing change from the fast paced life, which they had left behind. They had traveled from Dublin down to Wicklow. Then further down to Waterford, a place renowned for its crystal ware. After a week's break, they traveled on to Cork and stayed another week at Castletownsend. A small place set in a little bay, surrounded by charming coves and tidal loughs.

Elena had become enthralled by the scenic southerly coastline. She never strayed far from the coastal roads or sea, and spent most of her days walking bare foot along the sands, with the warm breeze blowing wispily through her long dark, wavy hair. The sea mesmerized her hypnotically, and she felt naturally drawn to its vast enchanting depths. Sensing somewhere deep in her soul, that this was the peace she had yearned for. Pagan too, enjoyed the long carefree walks on the many beaches. His padded furry paws relished the softness of the sand. There were so many interesting scents for him to follow, and sniff out in the rock pools. The magic of Ireland had captured their souls. Elena felt sure that she could live here forever. Yet they had only seen a little bit of this beautiful land so far. She sensed that there was still so much more ahead.

Elena had packed up supplies from a local shop that evening, before they had moved on again. Driving continuously through the night, they had come around from a southerly direction. They were now heading south-west to the Dingle Peninsula, in the county of Kerry. Elena enjoyed the quietness of the winding roads during the night, and she found that there was very little traffic about at this time. It was almost dawn as they arrived at Dingle. The bay was a spectacular sight swathed in an ethereal glow of half-light, which spread across the horizon. The light moved slowly as though heavenly gates were opening, heralding the dawn. Elena parked the van along the edge of the road, to one side of them were rolling green hills, and high mauve-grey mountains beyond, whose peaks reached into the sky. A grassy bank verge dropped dramatically from the road on the other side, and met with the long curve of golden sand edging the vast azure sea.

Elena poured herself a mug of tea from her thermos as she sat watching the dawn break. Just like a grand theatre performance, the sky line revealed the morning sun in its full glory. Then it slowly cast its light onto the sleepy contours of the land. "Now that is beautiful!" Elena said to Pagan; who sat in the passenger seat beside her. If he could talk Pagan would have replied. "But you've said that at every place in Ireland, which we've stopped at so far."

It was true she had said this often. There were so many precious moments to be had, and she felt privileged to see such wondrous sights. Pagan looked at her intently; he cocked his head to one side, and whined loudly. Elena glanced at him and then back at the landscape, feeling just a tinge of disappointment. She knew that as beautiful as Dingle was, it was still not the place in her dream. She sighed deeply and then finished her tea. Once again she made breakfast in the living quarters of the camper van. She had bought the van from a newspaper advertisement in England, and even though second hand it was still in good condition. It was well equipped on a small scale, and had a two ringed gas hob, which was sufficient for her needs. A single bed was built in, over the driver's cabin. There was a small sink with a cupboard, which stood opposite the mini table and seating space. They had mainly stopped at campsites, and she had managed well so far making use of the washing facilities on site. They hadn't faced any real hardship so far. She had kept a good stock of supplies, and even a first aid kit was stowed away for an emergency.

Elena hadn't much family left behind in England. Her father had left when she was five years old. Her mother had raised Elena, and her older brother single handedly. Her brother had married, and now lived happily in Staffordshire. Sadly her mother had died suddenly, quite unexpectedly from an acute asthma attack.

Elena's world had turned upside down, and for a while she had felt totally lost. She gave up her job, which she felt was a dead end; waste of her life. She kept in touch with her brother sending him postcards, and occasionally phoning him. He worried about her, but he knew his sister was far too headstrong to listen to him. Elena was indeed head strong and willfully wild at times. She had wondered if this was the reason why she hadn't married. She was already twenty five years old, and there had been a few marriage proposals from settled types of men. None of which she could have ever really loved, nor who could match her fiery, adventurous spirit.

Chapter Two

A young man by the name of Patrick James O'Neil waited nervously to meet his father, at his office in London. He sat perched on the edge of a plush leather chair, opposite a large highly polished rosewood desk. He felt anxious as he waited, and he tapped his slender fingers nervously against the hard wood desk. Patrick was twenty six years old, a grown man, and yet he still feared his overbearing father. His father, a very mature accomplished man was a top neurology surgeon, and well established in the medical field. He had always hoped or rather expected Patrick to follow in his footsteps, and become a surgeon too.

Patrick sat awkwardly trying to control his shallow breathing, while rehearsing his speech. He had gone over it a thousand times already in his mind. He glanced at his Rolex watch, which had been a gift from his parents. They had been exceptionally proud of him, when he had gained entry into medical school. The watch ticked in perfect time to his breathing, showing precisely ten seconds to eleven thirty. Patrick counted down the seconds mentally, and his stomach turned over. On the stroke of eleven thirty exactly, the office door burst open. His father, a tall grey haired man in a neat navy pinstripe suit, with a red silk pocket hanky, and matching silk tie entered the room.

Patrick leapt to his feet standing to attention as he always did when he met his father.

"Patrick my dear boy, how nice to see you." His father spoke rather loudly.

"Hello Father." Patrick uttered softly.

The older man walked briskly over to a side cabinet, muttering to himself, something incoherent. He took a large bottle of malt whiskey, and two crystal glasses and he set them down ostentatiously. "Care for one?" He asked pouring himself a rather large one.

"No thank you father." Patrick declined the offer.

He waited for his father to sit down, and take a large swig of his drink before he cleared his throat and began to speak. He told his father that he would like to take a year out of medical school. He explained that he didn't feel certain whether he really wanted to study medicine after all. Most importantly, he emphasized that he wanted to take time out to travel, to enable him to think clearly about his future, and what his other options might be.

The silence after he had spoken was just like the calm before the storm. He met his father's cold steel gaze reluctantly. For a moment his father's eyes seemed to glaze over, and then his voice exploded like a massive volcanic eruption. His whole face turned scarlet, red hot molten lava, and his voice boomed.

"Get out of my sight you worthless good for nothing. You are no son of mine. GET OUT!!"

Patrick felt his legs stand up, turn and walk as automated as a robot. He wanted to run, but his body wouldn't accept his brains command. He even stopped to close the door quietly on his way out. Patrick kept his eyes downcast unable to look up again, and see his father's furious out raged face. He left and walked away from the hospital building feeling nauseated. His father's words were still ringing in his ears. Feeling shaky and unsteady, he had a flash back to childhood, recalling that same sickening feeling. He had feared his father all those years ago, and it was exactly the same today.

Walking towards his black B.M.W convertible car, he opened the door and got in. Just sitting for a while, he waited for his erratic breathing, to calm down. Slowly taking deep breaths he regained his composure. What had he really expected from his father? He shook his head in disbelief and drove the short journey home.

Patrick lived very close to his parent's enormous mansion. They had built him his own annex apartment, in their two and a half acre grounds. He lived as they expected him to, in a luxurious controlled lifestyle. Neither of his parents had any idea of the inner loneliness he really felt.

Patrick had been sent away to an all-boys boarding school at a young age. He had studied hard and achieved excellent grades. Unfortunately, he was never really popular with the other boys there. So he had made very few friends in his school life, and had been very much a loner there. Afterwards while at university, he had literally spent all of his time studying. He didn't ever attend the wild orgy student parties. He was asked to at first, but refused adamantly. So then after a while, they stopped inviting him. Patrick became almost invisible during his time there.

Now at the weekends he stayed at home, watched movies or read books. His luxurious lifestyle was actually very dull. Patrick had never had a proper girlfriend, or any other sexual encounter. So he suppressed his frustrations, and saved his pent up energy for his medical studies.

Now surprisingly Patrick was extremely attractive. Behind his shy reserved middle class upbringing there was a good looking toned, and fit young man aching for passion. His deep blue eyes certainly had hidden depths, which were yet to be explored. It was his suppressed passion, which led him to have the recurring dream. It soon began to haunt his night time slumber. In his dream he was a confident popular young man, the very life and soul of the party. He was at a beach party, with a beautiful dark haired woman. His passion was finally unleashed as he made love to her wildly and uninhibited. They had wandered away from the party to be alone in the sand dunes.

The dream had become a regular occurrence lately. In his waking hours it had begun to distract him from his studies. His mind constantly wandered off as passionate thoughts invaded his waking mind. Somewhere deep in his heart he ached for the dreams to be real.

Patrick had made his very drastic decision to take time out, when he had suddenly realized, that he had never traveled anywhere, without his parents by his side. They had been to all the good tourist resorts abroad, in most countries of the world. Fabulous cruises, luxury apartments, five star hotels but always accompanied by his parents.

His mother was sitting in the garden when he drove his car up the graveled driveway. She waved a hand carelessly to him as she sipped her midday cocktail. Patrick wanted to ignore her and go straight to his apartment, which lay beyond another graveled pathway, across a wide expanse of lawn and herbaceous borders. He sighed deeply, and made his way towards her.

"Whatever's wrong dear?" She asked as she patted the vacant seat beside her.

Patrick sighed again as he sat down heavily. He took a deep breath and told her everything, and when he had finished she looked sadly into his anxious blue eyes.

"Don't worry darling, if that's what you really want to do. Let me have a think about things, and you leave your father to me. I'll soon talk him round." She announced confidently.

Patrick looked at his mother and smiled. "Okay mother." He said kissing her lightly on the cheek, although he couldn't quite see how? She would manage to talk his father round. He left her then and went to his apartment. Once inside, he immediately lay down on the soft, white leather sofa. He felt mentally exhausted, and had a thousand thoughts whirling around in his head. He drifted into a restless sleep, and lay there undisturbed for the rest of the afternoon.

Later Patrick woke with a start; there was a loud ring from the telephone on the side table. He rushed to answer it almost tumbling off the sofa.

"Hello mother." He spoke into the receiver.

"Were you asleep?" She asked.

"No, of course not, I was reading." He lied.

"Oh, well your father and I would like you to come up to the house. Dinner will be served at eight," She stated.

Patrick quickly looked at his watch, showing quarter to eight. "Okay." He answered although not really relishing the thought of another encounter with his father, but not wanting to offend his mother either.

"Don't worry, everything's in hand." His mother spoke gently, sensing his anxiety.

"Is it really?" Patrick queried slightly unsure.

"Yes dear, see you at eight." She replied, and then hung up.

Within the next ten minutes Patrick had shaved and showered. He now stood in his designer built walk in wardrobe, which housed his expensive collection of tailored clothes, and foot wear. He moved his hand quickly across the row of neatly ironed shirts, which the housemaid kept in pristine order for him. Patrick chose an azure blue shirt, and matched this with dark trousers.

After dressing he checked his appearance in the Cheval mirror, he hoped his parents would approve. He checked his watch, and then rushed out of the apartment hastily.

Patrick braced himself taking a few deep breaths, before entering, his parent's home. Once inside there was a long narrow hallway, which led to the main grand entrance hall. He walked slowly as if dreading every step, which would take him closer to seeing his father again. The large kitchen doorway stood open, and he glanced in to see cook putting the last finishing garnishes to a huge side of beef.

"At least the last supper will be a good one." Patrick joked; surprising himself to have found a strand of humor amongst the nerves.

Cook glanced up. "Good evening sir." She seemed pleased with herself as her beef had cooked nicely.

Patrick nodded in approval, while also trying to muster a smile.

He continued on to the main entrance hall passing the large library, and morning rooms. He saw that the heavy oak dining room doors were open wide, awaiting his arrival. Patrick gulped as he caught a glimpse of his father's tall stature, which was standing by the huge side board. He was helping himself to an aperitif. Just then the Grandfather clock struck eight o'clock, and Patrick stepped forward into the dining room.

"Hello dear." His mother said cheerfully.

He noticed his father looked a lot calmer. His face had thankfully lost that explosive scarlet colour. They sat down together around the large oval table; his parents always dined using the best china and silverware. Patrick spoke mainly to his mother, just polite small talk really. His father nodded and grunted now and then, but added little else to the conversation. When dinner was over, his mother stood up first. "Shall we go through to the sitting room, your father and I have something important to say to you Patrick." She announced.

They all walked together across the marble hallway to the large and spacious sitting room. Patrick felt his chest tighten, and at the back of his mind he felt sure that he knew what they were going to say. He sat down perched on the edge of the sofa, and watched as his father poured himself a large brandy from a glass decanter. With his glass full he walked over, and stood in front of the huge fireplace, with a vague expression on his face.

His mother broke the silence and spoke pleasantly. "Your father and I have decided that you need a holiday dear."

Patrick looked dumbfounded as this wasn't at all what he had expected. She continued. "So we are sending you alone, for one month, to your late grandmother's cottage in Galway in the west of Ireland." She seemed delighted with the idea, and then asked. "Do you remember the quaint little cottage, which your grandmother left to me in her will?"

"I think so." Patrick answered slowly.

"Well that's what we have decided will be best for you, a long holiday by the sea." She coaxed.

He looked at his father whose face had suddenly become stern again, and he realized that this was totally his mother's decision. Patrick also realized with a sinking feeling, that he would be expected to go back to medical school on his return.

Patrick sighed defeated. "Okay." He answered. He would be going away without them at least, he thought to himself as though he had just won a consolation prize.

"Good then that's settled." His mother smiled victoriously, and then she told him rather hastily that he would be leaving the very next morning. She had booked his flight that afternoon.

Patrick thanked his parents halfheartedly, and then left to go home and pack his suitcase.

Chapter Three

Meanwhile, Elena and Pagan had spent the whole day milling around Dingle. There were crowds of tourists as it was the holiday season. Furthermore most of them were trying to get a glimpse of the famous resident dolphin, which the locals had named Funghi. The dolphin had become semi tame over the years, and it had adopted Dingle Bay as its home.

Elena positioned herself amongst the excited throng who "Oohed and ahhed" whenever Fungi appeared, with his dome shaped head bobbing above the waves. His curved mouth was open wide as if laughing at the congregation of spectators. The crowd cheered rapturously as the dolphin flapped his flippers at them, and turned somersaults splashing into deep blue waters. Elena was delighted; it was a privilege to see

such a beautiful creature swimming freely. She resolved going onward to the sea front in order to purchase fish and chips for her supper. She also chose a commendable white wine, to accompany this. At which point she and Pagan returned to the camper van, which had been parked in a field, and overlooked the entire bay. On arrival to the field she noticed that there were a lot more people about. Cars, vans and caravans were parked up in rows. There were people who were busy setting up tents and awnings, while others sat relaxing in deck chairs and sun loungers.
"Hello" a woman spoke nearby as Elena approached her van.
Elena nodded and smiled back as she set about uncorking her wine, and finding glasses. She set out her deck chair, and offered the woman a glass of wine. She accepted it gratefully as she joined Elena

for a chat. The sunshine was incessant and it was a beautiful day. Anne introduced herself; she was a very curious person in a friendly sort of way. She asked Elena countless questions as she was genuinely interested in her unconventional lifestyle. Elena answered most of the questions, which Anne asked casually. When Anne discovered that Elena read fortunes with Tarot cards, she asked for a reading immediately.

Elena agreed to this, so she set up her little table and brought out her Tarot cards. She read for Anne easily, and she seemed content with the outcome. Anne pressed some money into Elena's hand and said. "Thank you."

Soon after, word had spread around the camp like wild fire. Suddenly a queue of people had formed outside Elena's van, all of them wanting a Tarot reading. By the end of the day she had made quite a tidy sum of money, although she hadn't really planned to spend her day that way, it had sort of just happened.

After stowing the money carefully away in a little Chinese tea caddy, Elena decided to take Pagan down to the bay for an evening walk. Dingle beach looked lovely, it's beautiful soft golden sand; lay against the shimmering turquoise sea. The sea breeze was cooler now as the sun began to sink gradually, over the distant horizon. The last of the surfers were coming out of the sea wearing tight black wet suits, and carrying large multi coloured boards. There were a few other people taking a stroll along the lengthy stretch of sand too. Some had dogs with them, while others were with small children and elderly people in their twilight years. Young lovers walked slowly hand in hand, stopping every now and then to kiss.

Elena walked in the wet sand right along the edge of the shore; she felt the cool sea water run over her feet as the tide had started to come in. Every now and then she stopped, and stooped down to pick up sea shells that glistened like treasure in the sand. Pagan ran backwards and forwards into the rippling waves, he loved the water, and was thoroughly soaked by now. Then as dogs do, he rolled over and over in the sand, which stuck to his wet coat. Elena laughed at him, and then said. "Come on we'll go back now."

Slowly they meandered up the winding lane to the campsite. They stopped briefly at a roadside water pump, where she made Pagan stand reluctantly under it, while she washed the sand off him. Immediately he shook himself doggy style soaking Elena in the wet spray. On reaching the campsite, she saw a hive of activity going on. People had set up barbeques and groups of traveling musicians were playing in the center of the field. Elena tied Pagan up at the side of her van, and then went to join the crowd.

Everyone seemed in good humor, and a few people were dancing to the lively music. Elena moved through to the front to get a better view of the group. The lead guitarist noticed her and winked cheekily. She smiled back. He was fairly good looking she mused to herself.

"He likes you!" A voice spoke. Elena turned to see Anne, the woman she had met earlier.

"Well he's okay." She laughed.

"Okay?" Anne asked surprised. "He's gorgeous. I wish my Frank looked like him."

Elena laughed again she had met Frank earlier, although he wasn't exactly attractive, he had seemed a good husband, and an excellent father to their three kids.

The evening wore on and the night air became very humid. Elena decided to go back to her van to change her clothes. The musicians were also taking a break, and food was being served at a large barbecue. Hot dog sausages and burgers sizzled away sending appetizing wafts through the evening air. The scents must have carried across the field to Pagan as Elena suddenly heard his distinctive high- pitched howl. She grabbed a couple of hot dogs quickly, and then started to walk away from the crowd.

"Not going so soon?" A husky voice asked. It was the guitarist; he was blond, tanned and gorgeous. He started to walk beside her as she headed across the grass towards the howling dog. He introduced himself as Dave, a cockney by his accent from London, England. Elena spoke pleasantly saying she enjoyed his music, but also saying very little about herself except telling him her name. Dave invited her over to his trailer after the concert that evening. He pointed over to a large deluxe mobile home, which was noticeable due to its size and grandeur.

Elena shrugged her shoulders off handedly. "Maybe" she said coolly.

"Okay." Dave smiled casually as he turned and headed back.

Elena tossed the hot dog to Pagan, and he wolfed it down whole. She went into the van and emerged a few moments later with towels, wash bag and clean clothes, which she carried over to the shower block. The facilities were very basic, but she felt suddenly relieved to discard her worn clothes, and stand naked under the warm shower spray. Elena washed her soft tanned skin, and shampooed her hair feeling invigorated and refreshed. Wrapping her long wet hair turban style, she quickly dried herself with the other towel.

  Then dressing herself in a cool white skirt and halter neck top, she applied the barest touch of make-up. Next unraveling her hair, she combed it through, casually letting it fall damp around her shoulders. She decided the breeze would dry it naturally anyway. Elena returned to her van and left her things there. Spreading her towels over a make shift washing line strung up between her van, and a gorse bush. She then set about feeding Pagan, and making sure he had a fresh bowl of water. He looked up at his mistress lovingly. "I'll see you later, don't wait up." She laughed, and patted his brown furry head.

Elena returned to watch the rest of the concert. Dave couldn't keep his eyes off her, but she pretended not to really notice. After they had finished playing, the musicians decided to go to the village pub to catch last orders. "Are you coming Dave?" One of them asked.

"No you go on." Dave replied inadvertently.

"Oh I see." The other man said casting his eyes in Elena's direction and grinning.

Dave walked over to where Elena was standing, and he asked her again if she would like to come to his mobile for drinks?

"Okay." She answered nonchalantly. They started to walk together across the field to where the sizable mobile was parked. Dave unlocked the door, and he invited her in, but she said she would prefer to sit out on the steps.

"That's fine." He shrugged and went inside to fetch two cans of beer from the fridge.

He handed one to Elena, and then sat down on the trailer steps beside her. The night sky was lit by a thousand jeweled stars, which illuminated the twinkle in Elena's dark eyes.

"Didn't you want to go with your friends?" She asked. Dave considered this for a moment, and then he replied. "Well I would rather sit here with a beautiful woman, even if she won't come into my luxurious trailer." Elena laughed, feigning modesty as they sat talking, and drinking a while longer.

He could certainly talk she found out, he had the gift of the gab where women were concerned. She liked this, and she found herself enjoying his company more as the night wore on. It was obvious he liked her although she wasn't sure if she liked him enough, to let him make love to her.

"Two ships passing in the night." Dave remarked.

"Yes something like that." Elena answered softly; as she let her words drift away into the cool night air. Dave moved in closer, putting his arm around her bare shoulders. "I could keep you warm." He whispered.

"Yes you could." She replied letting that too hang in the air.

"I don't suppose there's any chance of......a kiss?" Elena cut in breaking his sentence.

"Well yea a kiss." Dave said deflated as he got up.

Elena stood up too and he slipped his hands around her waist, and pulled her towards him. She felt the hard ripples of his toned body press against her. His lips met hers passionately, and lingered on the soft moist plumpness of hers. He held her against him tightly wanting her to feel his urgency, and how badly he wanted her right then. The kiss lingered as though captured momentarily, and the night sky cast a silhouette over their bodies as they embraced beneath the stars.

Gradually Elena pulled away, and Dave opened his eyes. She could sense that he wanted so much more, but he knew it wasn't going to happen. Sighing heavily Dave smiled at her. Elena started to walk away, and he stood there watching her go.

"I'll walk over with you." He called out.

"There's no need." She replied. A calm cool breeze blew through the air, and caught the strands of her long dark hair.

Dave looked for her first thing the next morning, but she had gone. There was no sign of Elena, her dog or the camper van, but just a vacant space in the field. They had already moved on.

Chapter Four

Patrick arrived in Ireland the next morning. His flight had been delayed a short while at the airport in London, but eventually it departed for Dublin. On arrival he collected his luggage, and headed out through the arrival doors, amidst a mass of other passengers. He walked confidently straight to a taxi rank. He got into the first car as he noted the driver's friendly face. Patrick handed him the note with the address in Galway.

"That will cost you a fortune!" The driver said taken by surprise.

"Don't worry I have enough money." Patrick said honestly.

The driver turned to look at him, giving him the once over he observed the fine clothes, and Rolex watch gleaming on Patrick's wrist.

"Right you are then." He was pleased with the enormous fare, which he would take. So they began their journey to White Rose Cottage, Doorus, in County Galway. The driver was not short of conversation as are most of the Irish in a pleasant friendly way. In the first hour or so they had managed to discuss Patrick's life story, including the heated conversation, which he had with his father. And which had led to his present circumstances. There had been a comfortable lull for the next hour or so as the driver now knew everything he needed to know. They stopped on route at a small garage, which had a cafe room at the side. After refreshments and filling the petrol tank, they were headed on again to GALWAY. It was well sign posted along the way.

Patrick nodded off on route; the driver's soft lilt had lulled him gently off to sleep. He had missed some fantastic scenery along the way as surely the West of Ireland is quite stunning. The driver had a mind to wake him, but decided to let the man sleep. God knows he is in need of peace with a father like that! The hours passed blissfully as the taxi trundled along, the winding roads into the west. The sky was a bright blue, and the afternoon sun was high up in the cloudless sky. It was one of those perfect summer days……that we can all recall.

On reaching Galway City Patrick woke up; he looked around and then smiled lazily. He had just had the most relaxing sleep. He felt refreshed and eager to get to his destination. The driver pointed out

various sights and landmarks, which were typical of all main cities. Patrick listened politely thinking up relevant questions to ask. They took the main N18 route out of the busy city, passing through the villages of County Galway's Oyster country. The Oyster festival was held hereabouts in September each year.
"Do ye like oysters?" The driver asked.
"Yes I do actually, with a glass of champagne." Patrick replied. The driver chuckled to himself.

They drove on passing Drumacoo church, which was an ancient stone building. The driver pointed this out in tour guide fashion. When they came to Kinvarra, the south easterly inlet of Galway Bay, he opened the car windows to take in the sea breeze. Kinvarra was a quintessential quayside village. "I've often come here for a holiday." The driver spoke fondly.

"It's delightful." Patrick replied as he noticed the little fishing boats, which were gently bobbing in the harbor. He felt suddenly relaxed as the sea breeze washed over him, lightly blowing his hair. Sitting back comfortably he began to yield to the slower leisurely pace of rural Ireland. The driver glanced at him in his rear view mirror, and smiled knowing well the beneficial charm of his beloved emerald isle.

After Kinvarra they drove out north-west on the peninsula, and came to Doorus, which at one time back in the eighteenth century had been an island. Now Doorus was a tiny village with only one shop and a pub. The driver stopped at the shop to ask for the directions to White Rose Cottage. The shopkeeper came out to look at Patrick; he smiled curtly, and then gave the driver directions.

They headed out of the village as instructed, traveling the short distance to the coastal road. After a minute or so the driver turned into a narrow laneway, passing by vibrant hedgerows of wild Fuchsia. He pulled up and stopped suddenly. "This is it." He seemed quite pleased at how easy it had been to find.

Patrick looked at the little gate entrance through the Fuchsia hedge. Beyond a short pathway he could just make out the white washed thatched roof cottage. "Okay, that's great thank you." He said absently and then remembered. "Oh how much is the fare?" "That will be just 350 euro, if you don't mind sir." After paying the fare and giving a generous tip Patrick got his cases from the boot; the driver helped him carry the luggage up to the front door. There was an iron- gate, which was a little rusty, and creaked as he pushed it open to go through. They got the first glimpse of the huge white rose bushes, which scrambled up the cottage wall. "Rustic." Patrick declared, and then as an afterthought he added. "Oh my God I hope it's got electricity?" He took on a sudden panic attack feeling wary of going alone into the unknown.

"Are you going to be alright?" The driver asked sensing his anxiousness.

"Yes of course, I'm sure I'll be okay thanks." Patrick tried to sound nonchalant, while regaining his air of confidence.

"Right you are then I'll get going, but if you have any problems the lady in the shop said you could call in, and she'd help if she can." The driver informed him, and then with a smile he made his way back to his car, and was soon gone.

Hastily Patrick rummaged for the cottage keys, which were in his luggage. He found two keys, which were on a brass ring. He pushed one into the rusty lock, turned it, and heard the little click as the door opened. Pushing it open wide he was pleasantly surprised to see it was clean and tidy inside, although rather a little old fashioned. His grandmother had lived to a great age before she had died. He remembered his mother's description of the quaint little cottage.

Patrick carried his luggage in, and then looked around to see where the bedroom might be. It was just off to the side of the sitting- room; there was a large Victorian brass bed, an antique wardrobe and a dressing table. These were the only things in the room, but it seemed sufficient. Patrick dropped his luggage in the bedroom, and went to explore the rest of the cottage.

In the kitchen he went straight to the cupboards to investigate, and to his surprise he found they were well stocked with supplies. Patrick began to relax as his vision of a dingy, cobwebby, derelict place started to evaporate. "This could be nice." He spoke calmly.

Next he unpacked his portable C.D player, and put on some classical music. Pottering around he opened other cupboards and a door, which led to a small sitting room complete with floral sofa, and some kind of radio. There was an open fireplace with a stack of logs, which sat in a basket on the stone hearth. The kitchen was off to the side of this room, and it had an old Belfast sink. A pine dresser stood against the far wall, and there was also a very strange looking cooker. Patrick found there was another bedroom, which contained a single brass bed, but nothing else. That was the extent of the cottage, so he wondered to himself, where the bathroom might be?

Could it be through the door in the kitchen? He went to ascertain, but it was locked. So using the second key on the brass ring he opened the door, which went straight out into the back garden! Patrick stepped through, and came out into brilliant sunshine. The fresh air cursed through his airways as he took deep inhalations of the sweet sea breeze. Towards the end of the long garden he noticed a white picket fence, which had a small wooden gate set into it. Patrick walked towards it curiously and when he got there he gasped! The view, which lay beyond the fence, was absolutely stunning; a wide stretch of beach met the azure blue sea way down below.

The cottage garden was actually at the top of a steep hill, which overlooked the bay. He couldn't resist it, and opened the little wooden gate immediately. There was a grassy bank and a meandering pathway which descended to the beach. "WOW!" Patrick shrieked in excitement just like a child. He felt compelled to rush straight down the winding path, so he started to run swiftly to get to the sandy beach. It was as though the sea were beckoning him, whispering his name on the fresh salty breeze. When he got down to the beach, Patrick pulled off his shoes and socks, instantly feeling the soft golden sand underfoot. He rolled up his trouser legs and unbuttoned his shirt, exposing his chest to the wind. It felt exhilarating; suddenly he was as care free as a child. He couldn't resist and ran straight into the sea shouting wildly as the waves rushed towards him. "This is fantastic." He shouted at the top of his voice, not caring a hoot as the beach was deserted anyway. Patrick spent a couple of hours on the beach splashing around in the sea, and exploring the many caves and rock pools. When he finally tore himself away he returned to the cottage. His energy was spent and he felt an overwhelming hunger. He was famished in fact as the sea air invariably had this effect.

Just then Patrick noticed the large tin bath, which was hanging on a nail outside the back door. "You've got to be joking?" He spoke aloud in utter disbelief. He laughed as he went inside, and decided to wash in the Belfast sink instead. So minutes later he had stripped off his wet clothes, and he stood naked as he waited for the kettle to boil. There suddenly came a loud knock at the front door. Patrick jumped quite startled, and then to his horror he heard a key turn in the lock as someone called out. "Hello it's only me, are you decent?" A woman's voice asked.

"NO! NO I'M NOT!" Patrick shouted in alarm, he grabbed the nearest thing to hand, which was a linen tea towel with Irish wild birds printed all over it. Mrs. Ryan stood in the doorway as Patrick made a mad dash past her, and straight into his bedroom.

"Oh I see." She apologized and went into the kitchen to wait.

Meanwhile in the bedroom Patrick gasped for breath as he grabbed a towel from his suitcase. He frantically rubbed himself dry, and then dressed quickly. He emerged flustered and red faced from the bedroom. The dark haired lady introduced herself as Mrs. Ryan, the housekeeper.

"Oh I see." Patrick responded, but he was still a little unsure whether she should have just let herself in. Either way she wasn't fazed by his unusually shy demeanor. Mrs. Ryan turned out to be most helpful in showing Patrick how to work the old Stanley range cooker. Patrick was delighted to see that she had brought a nice beef casserole with her. "Can't have you cooking for yourself, you poor wee man, not on your first day here now can we?" She soothed in her strong Irish lilt as she lit the range, and then put the cooked casserole on the top to heat up.

"Give it a while to warm and then taste it." She advised, and then asked him if there was anything he needed to know?

"Yes actually there is something, where's the toilet? There is one isn't there?" Patrick asked looking slightly concerned.

"Of course there is!" Mrs. Ryan answered laughing out loud. Then she sensed his awkwardness and her voice softened. "It's there just outside at the side of the house."

"Oh I see, thank you." Patrick said politely. Thinking this situation was totally alien to him. Mrs. Ryan left a short while later saying she'd call again. "There's really no need I think I'll manage." Patrick said kindly. Mrs. Ryan wouldn't hear of it and repeated that she would call again.

"Oh well ok then," he sighed, not really fussed one way or the other. He went to the bedroom where he put on some music, and lay down for a while. Soon he drifted away into a relaxed sleep, dozing calmly.

He woke up half an hour later as wafts of bubbling, hot casserole greeted him. Mrs. Ryan grew in Patrick's estimation as he consumed the delicious tender beef, and country vegetables in rich gravy. He actually licked his plate clean, it really was that good.

Then he got up and left everything as it was on the table. He went into the sitting room there wasn't a television, but instead an old radiogram stood in the corner. Patrick discovered curiously that it still worked, and he spent the rest of the evening listening to a country station, which played old Irish ballads.

Chapter Five

Elena had driven for the most part of the day. From Dingle Bay she'd headed up to county Clare, where she had stopped at a place called Lahinch. Here at a surfer's beach she had lunch at a small restaurant, which overlooked the sea. Although it was nice there she was eager to move on, so didn't bother finding a campsite. She felt restless today as though some unknown force were guiding her. Something was telling her to keep moving, but she wasn't quite sure what it was that was driving her on. She just had an intuitive feeling.

Pagan sensed it too, and he only got out of the van once to relieve himself. He sensed there wouldn't be a long walk on the beach for him here. He sat beside her in the passenger's seat as he waited for her to start the engine. Elena glanced at him, he was wearing his red bandana around his neck, and this made her smile. She turned the ignition key, it started up first time, and they were soon reversing onto the road again.

From Lahinch they stayed on the coastal road and drove around the Burren headland. The famous cliffs of Moher were to the side of the coastal road, with its sheer dramatic drop of 660 foot at the highest point above the Atlantic Ocean.

By now mid –afternoon the roads had become very busy with holiday- makers. Elena became impatient to get out of Clare, but the camper van unfortunately was not built for speed. They drove on and the road became less congested as they passed Doolin. They passed by around Fanore and the Black headland. The scenery was truly outstanding. Elena started to relax once more and go with the flow.

A good stretch later and they had crossed into the county of Galway. Elena instantly had a strange feeling of déjà vu. "Maybe I've been here in another life?" She said jokingly glancing at Pagan. They reached the small quayside village of Kinvarra, where she stopped and parked the camper van. There were a few boats bobbing gently on the water where they were moored. A mix of people was milling around the quayside, and a band of musicians were playing live music.

Elena walked towards a seafood restaurant, which was lit up and looked welcoming a short way along the quay. The waiter seated her at a small bistro table, which had a floral oil cloth and a small glass vase, with artificial carnations in it. She chose an oyster dish and a glass of white wine from the menu. After a short waiting period, she was served a large oval platter that looked sumptuous. It was laden high with oysters on a bed of fresh salad. The sea air was salty and left its taste on her lips, and a briny smell penetrated her nose. The cool white wine was refreshing, but left her just a little light headed.

"That was lovely." She said as she smiled at the waiter appreciatively. She had finished half a dozen shelled oysters, and sipped the last of her wine draining the glass completely. Elena paid her bill and left a tip for the friendly waiter. She then strolled back to the van at a leisurely pace. There she fed Pagan and afterwards put his lead on, and they walked together back along the quayside.

Later she decided to drive on just a little further, Kinvarra was a lovely place, but something pulled at her soul. "You are almost there; the wind whispered to her." An involuntary shiver ran up Elena's spine, and she shuddered. Pagan looked up at her, his senses on high alert. They drove on along the winding coastal road which was almost deserted. The headland stood out as a dark silhouette against the approaching evening sky. There was a strange air of foreboding, but the mystery of a new place was enough to lure them on. When they had reached Doorus, which was on the small peninsula Elena had another strange feeling. It was a sort of butterflies in the stomach fluttering kind of feeling. "My God Pagan, I think this is it!" She laughed excitedly and Pagan barked loudly.

They turned off the main road and drove down a winding lane. The hedgerows here were thick with little pink droplet flowers of wild Fuchsia. They passed an isolated cottage along the winding country lane. "Oh that's pretty!" Elena remarked on the white washed cottage, which had huge white roses growing up against its walls. They drove on slowly now and presently came to a sandy beach cove.

Elena watched the waves curl and roll up over the sand, and it had a natural calming effect. On one side of the cove a meandering pathway wound its way up the side of a steep grassy hill. To the other side a densely covered hill rose up against the skyline.

Elena reversed the van slowly back up the narrow winding road, she hoped they wouldn't meet any cars coming down. They didn't luckily and halfway back up she turned off to the right. There was another narrow road, which went past a thick pine forest. After a short distance she noticed a small farmhouse, and she stopped to investigate.

"Hello there." She heard a friendly voice call out as a middle- aged man walked towards her. Elena greeted him and then asked whether he knew of anywhere she could camp for a while?

The man introduced himself as Mr. Ryan. He said she could park on his land for a small fee. "Great!" Elena replied, she was delighted at her good luck. She immediately went to fetch her money from the Chinese tea caddy.

"Will you be staying long?" Mr. Ryan enquired. "Yes I think I will." Elena replied. So Mr. Ryan arranged for her to pay by the week. He showed her to the spot in his field where she could set up camp. He also told her that she was welcome to use the outside facilities of the farm, which were a toilet and small wash- room. She thanked him gratefully, and he left her to get organized.

Elena decided to wash a few clothes first, and she set up a line from the side of the camper van window across to the thick hedgerow. She took a small bundle of clothes to the wash room; it was basically a stone building, which housed a large Belfast sink. She hand washed the clothes, and then pegged them out neatly in the light evening breeze.

It was getting quite dark now, so they postponed the expedition to the beach until morning. "We'll get up really early and go then." She informed Pagan. She made up her bed leaving the curtains open, so she could see the stars forming constellations in the night sky. Elena lay down and listened to the portable radio, which played old Irish ballads. Elena felt sure this was the place from her dream as she felt butterflies flutter in her stomach. She got up from the bed feeling suddenly restless, so she reached into the cupboard and pulled out a small wooden box. It was made of rosewood and it was beautifully carved. In the center of the lid there was an ornate symbol of a sword, which impaled a rose.

Elena spread a piece of black cloth on her bed and sat crossed legged in front of it. She opened the box and withdrew her pack of Tarot cards. She held them for a few moments, and recited an incantation quietly almost whispering. Shuffling the pack she stopped instantly when she felt them click. She spread out ten of the cards; face down in the formation of the Celtic cross, and put the rest of the pack to one side.

Elena took a deep breath as she began to turn over the cards one by one, and see what they were about to reveal. After turning the last three she gasped quite visibly startled. This wasn't what she had expected to see. Elena immediately gathered all of the cards together, and she put them back into the box hastily. She decided then to make some tea as she felt this would help to calm her nerves. Elena spent the rest of the evening sitting outside on the camper van steps, sipping her tea as she gazed at the night sky all lit up with stars.

The Tarot cards began haunting her thoughts, especially Le Maison Dieu and La Mort. Many years of studying their symbolism had taught her, they were definitely not for the feint hearted. She sighed deeply, sensing the dark shrouded veil closing in. Up to this point she had felt optimistic, finally she had dared to hope of meeting her true love, the man of her dreams. All of a sudden she felt lost and so very alone.

Chapter Six

Patrick had woken very early in the morning. He had leapt out of the old brass bed as soon as he had opened his eyes. The unfamiliar surroundings hadn't fazed him at all, on the contrary he felt at home here oddly enough after only one night. He rummaged through the drawers of the old dressing table, and he pulled out a pair of swimming shorts. All of a sudden he remembered that Mrs. Ryan might just walk in again at any moment, so he stood with his back pressed firmly against the bedroom door. Patrick struggled to remove his boxer shorts and wiggle into the swim wear. He left the boxer shorts exactly where they lay on the floor. Next he grabbed a large beach towel from the top shelf of the wardrobe. At that point Patrick walked through the kitchen passing the sink full of last night's dinner plates, casserole dish and cutlery. With his towel rolled under his arm, he breezed out through the back door of the cottage.

The morning sunshine dazzled bathing the whole garden with its warm rays. The air carried a sweet smelling musky fragrance from the huge white rose blooms. Everything gleamed brightly with the fresh scent of morning. Patrick walked to the end of the garden quickly, and as the view of the sea greeted him he drew in a deep breath. "Beautifully stunning, absolutely fantastic," were his first words of the new day. He opened the gate and sauntered through to the winding sandy track, which lay before him. Patrick walked down gingerly minding his feet on the stones as he went. He hadn't bothered to put any shoes on in his eagerness to get outdoors.

He heard a dog bark suddenly down below on the beach. Patrick stopped in his tracks abruptly quite startled. He couldn't see the dog at first, and then as he surveyed the horizon he noticed something moving out at sea. Shading his eyes with his hand he strained against the bright sunlight to see what it was. Someone was swimming out there, and then the dog appeared barking excitedly as it ran along the shore.

Patrick felt instantly annoyed as if whoever the person might be, were a trespasser on his idyllic beach. He huffed as he started to walk down slowly, his mood now mixed and deflated. He wondered whether he should turn around and go back to the cottage. Maybe he should wait until whoever it was came out of the sea, and went away. Then realizing he didn't really want to go back, but it was just how startled he felt then he decided to carry on.

Patrick saw the person now swimming towards the shore. He felt suddenly curious to see who it was so he continued to walk forwards slowly. The swimmer emerged from the sea, and Patrick looked on in astonishment and his jaw dropped gaping. She walked out of the rippling waves like a goddess. Her tanned curvaceous body was clad in the skimpiest white bikini, which barely covered her. She walked towards him as the sunlight caught the water droplets on her skin, which gleamed like pure gold.

Patrick's mind went numb; he could just manage to close his gaping mouth as she came up to him.

"Hi." Elena said smiling at him.

"Hello." Patrick struggled to force the word out, but then he managed to smile too. His gaze went down the full length of her body and then up again. His eyes fixed on her protruding nipples, which showed visibly through her wet bra top. Patrick blushed instantly turning a deep crimson red as he felt a strong stirring in his groin. He had never before in his life ever been this close to such a beautiful, exotic, bikini clad woman. He looked up at her focusing on her face as he quickly held his towel in front of him. He tried desperately to hide his reaction.

"Are you visiting here?" He asked trying to sound casual.

"Yes." She answered breezily. Just then Pagan came bounding towards them covered in sand, he wagged his tail enthusiastically.

"Is this your dog?" Patrick asked, but he immediately thought it was a dumb question.

"This is Pagan." She announced as she patted the dog's head playfully. Pagan sniffed Patrick's legs, and then sat in front of him looking up, while panting and letting his big, wet, sloppy tongue fall to the side of his mouth. "He likes you." Elena laughed.

"Oh that's good." Patrick replied as he too patted the dog's large head gingerly.

"Well we had better be going." She stooped to retrieve her sandals and beach towel.

"Oh." Patrick seemed a little dismayed.

"Enjoy your day." She smiled and then headed off towards the laneway. Patrick watched her go, just then realizing he hadn't even asked her name. He really was that shy, although the image of her coming out of the sea was firmly tattooed in his mind. He could not imagine how that image would haunt him as time went by. As soon as Elena was out of sight, Patrick ran quickly straight down into the sea. The waves rolled refreshingly cool against his hard, hot body, and he started to swim easing all his tension.

He let the rhythm of the waves invigorate him. Patrick was a strong swimmer, and he swam regularly at home in his parent's pool. It seemed tame when compared to the wildly exciting Atlantic Ocean. He was unaware that Elena had stopped and that she was now watching him swim. She stood with her beach towel draped around her and gazed out at the lone swimmer.

She hadn't asked him his name because she didn't have to. She already knew him; he was the man she had seen in her visions and dreams. So why was she walking away when they had only just met?
Well because she was playing it cool as any intuitive female does, and she knew what lay before her.

Elena and Pagan returned to the camper van, which was in farmer Ryan's field. She washed and changed into a light cotton dress, and rinsed out her swimwear.

She hung it to out to dry on her makeshift line. Afterwards she cooked breakfast consisting of bacon, eggs, sausages, black and white pudding, and tomatoes. Her swim in the sea this morning had certainly aroused a voracious appetite.

Meanwhile, Patrick had finished his swim and headed back up to White Rose Cottage, via the winding, sandy track. The sea had given him a hearty appetite too, and he started to think about breakfast.

Patrick entered through the back door of the cottage, and he got quite a start when he saw Mrs. Ryan there. She was standing in the middle of the kitchen with her hands firmly on her hips. She looked more than a little annoyed and flustered. "Good morning!" She snapped no trace of her previous friendly tone. Patrick didn't understand her clipped speech at first. He followed her gaze towards the sink, where his dirty plate and casserole dish were stacked up.

"Oh." Patrick remarked, unsure whether she was supposed to wash those or not? Or indeed whether she had expected him to? In his home the maid did this kind of work.

"Right I see how it is!" Mrs. Ryan remarked. She could never stay angry for any longer than a minute or so. Her features softened just a little as she spoke again. "Look I expect you're hungry? So I'll make a deal with you. When you've changed out of your wet things, you can wash last night's dishes. I will cook you a nice fried breakfast. Ok my dear?" She hadn't paused once for Patrick to interrupt or voice an opinion. "Okay Mrs. Ryan." He replied, and then went straight into the bedroom to change. Afterwards he came back to the sink, and filled it with water. Patrick began by dipping the cutlery in.

"Saints preserve us! Did you forget the washing up liquid? The scourers are under the sink dear." Mrs. Ryan chuckled as she tossed bacon rashers, lightly into the hot frying pan on the range.

"Yes of course." He searched for them at once, then squeezing nearly half the bottle of liquid into the sink. He proceeded to dunk the dishes as soapy foam bubbles splashed onto the tiled floor.

"No!" Mrs. Ryan shrieked as she dropped the white pudding suddenly into the frying pan.

"Sweet Jesus, Mary and Joseph, God forgive me! Did you ever do anything for yourself at home?" She raised her voice in anger, and slammed the pan to one side.

"No actually I didn't." Patrick replied honestly suddenly feeling clumsy, and ignorant. She looked at him for a moment then, and realized just how silver spoon in the mouth he really was. She tutted to herself and then muttered something along the lines of "we'll soon change that my boy." She told him calmly to put more water in the sink, and to be sure to rinse everything really well afterwards. She continued to explain how she had lit the range cooker, with kindling wood, firelighters and peat briquettes. She talked very slowly as if talking to an eejit, and emphasized every word. She hoped he was retaining this valuable information, which she was sharing with him. Mrs. Ryan placed a perfect fried egg alongside the bacon rashers, white pudding, sausages, hash browns, potato bread and wild mushrooms. It looked and smelt delicious, and Mrs. Ryan noted the appreciative smile on Patrick's face.

"There you go now." She set the plate down on the table. There was a fresh white Irish linen cloth and cutlery already set out for him. "Will you be dining with me?" Patrick asked as he sat down to his feast. "Me? Oh no dear. I already ate my breakfast at home with Mr. Ryan. He's a farmer you see, and we're always up very early." She had a little gleam in her eye as she talked lovingly about her husband of forty years. She did sit down with Patrick, and take a cup of tea from the Willow pattern china tea set. They chatted away, and Mrs. Ryan accepted that it wasn't exactly Patrick's fault he wasn't domesticated. There had always been maids, and other staff to attend to that side of things. Mrs. Ryan listened intently as he described his upbringing and home life. She asked politely. "Did you never think of finding yourself a nice girl to marry, and settle down with?"

"Not really. I mean..." He let his words trail off. Suddenly an image of the girl on the beach flashed into his mind. He blushed and looked down at his plate as he finished the last remains of the breakfast. "Thank you that was the best breakfast, I've ever had."

"You're welcome, so now soak the plate in hot soapy water, and we'll make a start on the bedroom." Mrs. Ryan was beaming inside; she secretly enjoyed receiving praise for her cooking skills.

They went into the bedroom, and she immediately opened the little glass paned window, "to air the room." She smiled while instructing him again adopting the eejit tone. Between them they straightened out the bed, while he gathered up the wet clothes from the floor, and put them into a bag.

"Come on then I have a little surprise for you." Mrs. Ryan informed Patrick. He followed her out of the door, and carried the bag of clothes as instructed.

They walked together down the laneway about one hundred yards or so. Then they turned off to the left and headed for Home Farm. This was where Mr. and Mrs. Ryan lived. They came towards the grey stone gateway, and walked over the metal cattle grid. Patrick noticed the camper van, which was parked in the side field. "Is that your van?" He asked.

"Oh no that belongs to a young lassie from England." Mrs. Ryan replied.

"Does it?" Patrick seemed genuinely surprised.

"Yes she's probably down at the beach with her dog. She spends a lot of time at the beach." Mrs. Ryan replied. Patrick's mind suddenly sprang into action as he remembered the woman, whom he had met that morning. His heart began to pound in his chest as he recalled her scantily clad body.

"Do you know her name?" Patrick took a couple of deep breaths trying to sound casual, and slow his racing heartbeat.

"Elena is her name." Mrs. Ryan replied noticing the little spark in Patrick's deep blue eyes. She said no more about Elena. She led the way as she went into the farmhouse and off through a side door, which led into the utility room.

"There you are dear; this square thing is known as a washing machine." She announced but then smiled. She showed him how to separate his light from his colored clothes. Then how to put in the soap powder and conditioner in and lastly to set the wash dial to the required cycle. She spoke to him very slowly as if he were a complete imbecile. The first wash would take at least thirty minutes or so. Patrick decided to take a look around the farm to pass the time.

Just then as he came out of the house his heart skipped a beat, when he saw Elena. He summoned up the courage, and shouted over to her hastily. "Hello." Pagan emerged from the van, and ran towards Patrick barking in a friendly greeting. Pagan sensed this was a nice human. "Hello." Elena smiled as he came towards her, with the dog sniffing at his heels. She spread out a large checked travel rug on the grass, and sat down stretching out her long tanned bare legs. Patrick felt a little bit awkward, but instinctively knelt down beside her. "So what brings you here?" Elena aske asked. "Oh I'm just doing my washing." Patrick wished instantly, that he had a more interesting excuse to be at the farm.

"Great I like a man who can fend for himself." She spoke in a friendly tone, and laughed lightly. Patrick laughed too, and soon felt at ease in her company. They sat talking for a while, just getting to know one another. He found her very attractive, and felt sure it was mutual; by the way she looked into his eyes as she spoke to him. Also by the way she tilted her head slightly as she listened to him. He felt as if she could see into the core of his soul, and sense his deepest, darkest desires. He wanted her to see every desire……..

"You're washings done." Mrs. Ryan's familiar Irish accent broke the spell. Patrick got up quickly. "I better go." He seemed reluctant, and he desperately wanted to ask her out to dinner or something. He also knew he would die, if she refused his offer. So he didn't say anything as his courage had deserted him. "I don't suppose you would like to join me later for a barbeque on the beach?" Elena asked him by chance. "Oh yes that would be great! Thanks I mean I would love to." Patrick stumbled over his words he couldn't believe his luck. "Okay see you there at eight." Patrick nodded and blushed as he realized his clumsy manner. He walked quickly over to the farmhouse once more with his heart pounding in his chest. When he got inside he punched the air and shouted "Yes!" Mrs. Ryan watched his strange antics and laughed, before instructing him how to unload the wash, and put the next one on. "Now take these home and peg them straight out on the line." She handed him the bag of washed clothes.

As he passed Elena on his way out he waved to her. "See you at eight." His new found confidence now showing in his manner, she nodded and waved back.

When he got back to White Rose Cottage Patrick went straight out, and hung the washing in the garden. Then he went inside and tackled the washing up. "There's nothing to it really." He said triumphantly when he had finished. Pleased with the little stack of plates, cups and saucers, which he had left to dry on the wooden drainer. He suddenly remembered the frying pan, so he emptied it and washed this too. He took the Irish linen cloth, dusted the crumbs onto the floor, and pegged this out on the line too.

Patrick glanced at the clock, where he saw that there were still few hours to go until the barbecue on the beach. He wondered aimlessly around the cottage not really knowing how to pass the time. So he decided to ring his mother, and see how she was. He kicked off his shoes, and sprawled out on the brass bed as he idly pressed the numbers on his phone. His mother answered promptly, she seemed delighted to hear his voice. They chatted for a long time, mostly about his father, the garden party that she was planning, the guests she had invited, and other mundane topics. It seemed very odd, that his mother didn't once enquire what he had been doing. Patrick thought this a little strange, but didn't mention it. He thought that perhaps she had too many other things on her mind. "Okay mother I'll ring you tomorrow." He announced before he hung up.

Afterwards Mrs. Ryan arrived at the cottage with the second lot of his washing, which was folded neatly in a bag. "We were wondering if you would like to come up to the farmhouse for your dinner this evening." She asked.

"Oh thanks very much for the invite, but I'm going to a barbecue on the beach." He replied, and sounded excited. She nodded. "I see, well you have a nice time dear." She went out into the garden with the bag of washing. Suddenly he heard her roaring with laughter. Great peels rang out loudly, and she was quite hysterical. Patrick rushed outside, where he saw the washing strewn all over the hedge and the white picket fence, which he had pegged out earlier. "Your pants are down there on the beach." Mrs. Ryan couldn't stop chuckling; as she helped him to retrieve what was left. At which point she showed him how to peg them on the line firmly. Patrick thanked her profusely as they returned to the house. Once inside he waited for her to notice the washing up.

"Well there's hope for you yet." She smiled broadly at him. "Now I must get going, I've got plenty to do at home." She let herself out of the front door and departed.

Patrick glanced at the clock again, and then decided to make himself a sandwich; sure he could manage this task with ease. He took bread from the wooden bread bin, and ham from the fridge. He slapped one cold slice between two pieces of bread. He went out into the garden again carrying his sandwich on a plate.

The weather was so bright and sunny, with not a single cloud in the clear blue sky. He found an old wooden deck chair leaning against the outside wall, which was a bit battered and worn, but he didn't mind this. He set it out on the lawn, and settled himself comfortably in it to sunbathe. Patrick watched his washing flap to and fro in the warm breeze, and his thoughts turned to this evening and Elena.

Chapter Seven

By quarter to eight Patrick had already changed his outfit several times. He was very nervous as it was his very first date, and he wanted to look right. He'd tried the navy shirt and dark trousers, but decided he looked too formal, so discarded them lazily onto the floor. These were soon joined by the other half of his wardrobe as he soon began to feel flustered, and anxious. At last his light blue shirt and black jeans seemed to be the perfect look casual, but not too casual. He raced from the house down to the bottom of the garden towards the picket fence, and the wooden gate. As he went through the gate to the sandy track, Patrick saw the wisps of smoke coming up from the beach. There she was, he saw her down on the beach, and his heart flipped over.

He got to the bottom of the track, quickly pulling off his shoes and socks as he walked barefoot towards her. She had the travel rug spread out on the sand beside a small barbeque, which had an array of burgers and steaks cooking away. There was a bottle of wine uncorked, and ready to pour into two glasses, which stood side by side.

"It's nearly ready." Elena smiled as she turned the steaks over on the smoldering charcoal. Patrick sat down on the rug, and accepted the glass of Burgundy wine. She watched him sip his wine as he tasted its full- bodied flavor. She casually took in his well-toned muscular shoulders, which were outlined beneath his blue cotton shirt. His gaze took in her shapely curves as she leaned forward to set out plates, and cutlery before him. Their eyes met for a moment, and Patrick felt hypnotized by her dark brown eyes.

"I think they're ready." Elena smiled breaking the moment instantly. She served him a large steak offering him French fries, and salad to go with it. She topped up their wine glasses, and they sat and ate as the sea lapped gently against the shore.

It was a beautiful evening, and the sky had now changed colour from light blue to deep shades of pink, with streaks of dark orange. The large golden disc of the sun had set high in the western sky. It cast the last of its rays like long fingers stretching to their full length, which reached the distant horizon. A final curtain call to its audience of land and sea it lingered, and seemed reluctant to give way to the moon, which waited in the wings. The sea was calm on its surface; the vast expanse of water shimmered, and sparkled as the sun lightly caressed the gentle waves in a fond farewell.

They had finished eating, and spent a good part of the evening talking. Now they watched as the golden Sun began its descent. Elena had gradually moved closer sensing Patrick's lack of experience. He didn't move away when she moved closer to him on the rug, but he began to chatter nervously. Elena knelt in front of him deliberately, and put her finger to his lips. "Shush!" She whispered and then kissed him very softly. As she pulled her mouth away she looked intently into his eyes. She saw the unmistakable desire secretly smoldering away in his virginal heart. She kissed him again, but this time more passionately, and he responded urgently as his body hardened. The motion of the sea became suddenly restless, and the pale moon rose up high in the night sky.

Elena undressed Patrick slowly, and then made him wait as she caressed his exposed chest lightly. Her lips lingered as she worked her way down his body. Patrick groaned loudly, and he felt sure he was going to explode at any second. He felt a deep needing ache, which began to throb, and he pulled suddenly at his jeans eager to be free of them. As he wrestled to get his long legs out of the tight jeans, Elena undressed effortlessly, and cast off her light cotton skirt. She unbuttoned her black lace bodice, which she threw carelessly onto the sand. Their nakedness was exposed beneath the pale full moon, and she gently pushed him to lie down in the soft sand. She caressed his body as she moved slowly stretching her legs over him. Patrick groaned deeply in anticipation. His head throbbed in time with his pulsating manhood, and he struggled to control his emotions.

The sea came in towards the shore, and then built up in motion as the waves swelled to their fullest height, out in the darkening deep waters. Patrick felt the wild sensation as he entered her body, and they became one. He gasped in euphoric elation, and then moaned as Elena moved on top of him to the rhythm of the tempestuous sea.

The waves carried their frothy white spray, which splashed onto the wet golden sand. Patrick came suddenly in a wild passionate explosion. When their emotions were finally spent, they lay together naked their bodies entwined in embrace. Elena listened to Patrick's erratic breathing, which slowly calmed as the tide began to draw back from the shore. The cool breeze whispered to the twinkling stars above. She covered them with the travel rug, and they slept soundly together until dawn.

When Patrick awoke all alone with only the travel rug covering him, he felt sure it must have been a fantastic dream. Then in the distance he saw her swimming out in the sea, at least he hoped it was her. She was swimming too far out for him to see clearly. Patrick strained his eyes as he tried to make certain it was Elena. He reached for his clothes, and dressed quickly leaving his shirt casually unbuttoned. He watched as she swam towards the shore. There was someone with her Patrick noticed right away as two heads bobbed in the moving water.

Pagan emerged from the sea first, and galloped towards Patrick like a mad dog. Pagan ran straight at him barking loudly in greeting, and then shook his sopping wet coat all over Patrick before jumping up and licking his face. Patrick was just about to tell the dog off, but then his attention was immediately distracted as Elena emerged from the sea. She was stark naked, and his eyes took in every inch of her golden tanned body; capturing the moment he smiled, and drew in a deep breath. He was at a loss for words, and so he just watched as she took a towel from her rucksack, and began to dry herself. She seemed at ease with her nakedness, a carefree spirited ease. Patrick had never in his life expected to fall in love at first sight. He felt like a real man at last now that he had cast off his virginal shroud he felt happier, and a little more confident.

As Elena dressed Patrick gathered up the empty wine glasses, and the remnants of their barbecue. They stood barefoot on the sand looking at each other; both were waiting, to see what the next move would be. He didn't know the meaning of a one- night stand, and she had no intention of letting it be just that! He noticed she had a glowing radiant look about her, and she noticed he had a more confident air.

"Well I'm going to go now." Elena said smiling.

"Can I see you later?" Patrick asked instantaneously.

"Yes sure." So they arranged to meet again later that evening. Elena walked away with Pagan following at her heels, and she felt butterflies flutter in her stomach.

Patrick stood waiting, and watched until they had disappeared along the laneway. He sighed heavily drawing in a deep breath. He made his way back up the sandy track to White Rose Cottage. It was still very early in the morning; and he wondered whether he should go straight to bed. He realized that wouldn't sleep so he decided not to bother. He grabbed the old tin bath, which hung on a nail on the wall at the back of the cottage. He carried it into the house and set it on the kitchen floor. It took him awhile to get the range cooker started, which would then heat the back boiler. So Patrick decided to fill the large kettle, and use saucepans as well. He filled them with water and placed these on top of the range to heat. While he was waiting he made tea and toast for himself. He sat down at the old kitchen table to eat. Eventually the water began to boil so he quickly went to fetch his towel, his wash things and the broom. He didn't want Mrs. Ryan coming in again, and catching him naked in the old tin bath. Patrick wedged the broom handle firmly against the front door. The large tin bath was only half full when he managed to get in it. Patrick wondered how his old grandmother had ever managed, with this primitive form of bathing.

Elena had gone back to Home farm; where she quickly made use of the wash- room shower. She saw Mr. Ryan's tractor drive out through the gates as she returned across the yard. Mrs. Ryan waved to her from the kitchen window; Elena waved back as she went through the field gate, to where her van was parked. Once inside her cozy little van she closed the curtains, and fell into bed. Pagan was sprawled flat out on the floor. They both slept soundly late into the afternoon.

Meanwhile Patrick had finished bathing, and he had emptied the old tin bath, which was now hanging back up on its nail outside. Mrs. Ryan had arrived at White Rose Cottage, and she was pleasantly surprised to see the range lit, and the breakfast things already washed up. She went in to tidy the bedroom, and noticed straight away that the bed hadn't been slept in. She quickly picked up the discarded clothes noting they were clean. She hung them carefully, and put them back in the wardrobe. Next she flicked her duster over the rose wood dresser, and then returned to the kitchen where Patrick was drinking tea.

"Would you like a cup of tea Mrs. Ryan?" He offered.

"Yes that would be nice." She looked at him shrewdly as she sat down beside him at the table. She noticed that he had learnt quickly the art of tea making. She also noticed the little carrier bag, which was by the kitchen door. "That's my dirty washing!" Patrick announced proudly.

Mrs. Ryan nodded then smiled, and said. "I'll take that for you dear."

"No, really it's okay, I'll bring it and do it myself thank you." Patrick replied eagerly as he wanted to catch a glimpse of Elena at Home farm. Mrs. Ryan eyed him suspiciously, so he added quickly. "I really do want to learn to do these things for myself."

She nodded again, and sipped her tea. After a few minutes had passed by she asked him casually, if he had enjoyed the barbecue last night. She added quickly "It was such a lovely evening did you stay late?"

Patrick faltered at first, and avoided her direct gaze. He mumbled something about taking a walk on the beach.

"That's nice dear." Mrs. Ryan finished her tea. She informed him, that she was going into the village to do a bit of shopping. Mrs. Ryan took a quick look into the cupboards and the fridge. She made a mental note of what shopping he might need, and then she left.

It was the middle of the afternoon when Patrick arrived at Home farm, clutching his carrier bag of washing in one hand, and two freshly cut white roses in the other. He walked past the farmhouse and straight into the field behind. He saw the camper van, and noticed the curtains were drawn across the side windows. He stood for a moment, and wondered whether he should disturb her or not? He decided to leave the roses by the door, and just then he heard a noise from inside the van. Patrick realized it must be Pagan as he then heard the dog sniffing at the bottom of the door. The dog recognized Patrick's scent, and he clambered up onto the small settee, poking his nose through the curtains. Patrick laughed at him and then walked over to the farmhouse. The rear door was open leading into the large homely kitchen, so he walked straight in. He continued through to the utility room, where the washing machine stood. He put his clothes in adding soap powder, and conditioner to the separate compartments. He set his wash at the same number as he had watched Mrs. Ryan do previously, and he pressed the knob in to start the cycle.

Patrick felt pleased with himself as he went to sit outside on the bench, which was under the kitchen window. He glanced over at the van, but there was no sign of Elena.

Just then Mrs. Ryan appeared carrying a few shopping bags. Mr. Ryan met her at the gateway as he parked his tractor. He was a grey haired man, with a weathered look about his features; Patrick noticed as they came towards him. Mrs. Ryan's eyes shone as she walked beside her husband proudly. She was still very much in love with him after many years of marriage. Patrick wished that his parents would show such devotion instead of the cold glances, which they frequently exchanged.

"Come in and have some dinner." Mrs. Ryan said to Patrick.

"Okay I will thanks." He followed them inside, where he was formerly introduced to Mr. Ryan, who shook his hand firmly. The two men soon get acquainted, and chatted easily as Mrs. Ryan waited on them. She served up a piping hot chicken casserole, which she had prepared earlier that morning.

The meal was delicious, and Patrick thanked them good heartedly before he went to collect his clothes, from the laundry room. He put the wet clothes into the bag, and walked quickly out of the farmhouse. He looked over the field gate to the camper van, but there was still no sign of movement. Just then Patrick noticed that the white roses were gone. He smiled as his thoughts flashed back to their night on the beach.

Chapter Eight

They met up later that evening on the beach, which was quickly becoming their familiar haunt. Patrick had arrived half an hour before the arranged meeting time. Elena arrived shortly after, and they were instantly at ease in each other's company. It seemed as though they had known each other a lot longer than just a day. They walked along the golden sand, their arms casually draped around each other's bodies. Their conversation was light as they strolled towards the sea, and the waves were gently lapping against the shore. Patrick asked if she had liked the roses, which he had left at her door. Elena replied telling him that she loved white roses; she felt they symbolized purity and peace.

They felt the cold sea water run over their bare feet as they stood still and kissed. The sinking sun cast a shadow over their silhouette on the sea shore. Elena shivered and a tingle ran the full length of her spine.

"Are you okay?" Patrick asked pulling his mouth from her soft moist lips.

"Yes, I'm fine." She replied lightly. They came away from the water, and walked over the wet sand to a long strip of beach. It had not yet been touched by the lapping waves, which were slowly creeping in with the tide. They walked around the headland and came to a tiny deserted cove. It looked very romantic as if it were kept only for secret lovers to explore. The rock face was very craggy, and dark crevasses lined its surface giving it an ancient eroded expression. There were many smaller caves cut into the rock at its base, and rock pools shimmered at the entrances. Patrick pulled Elena eagerly towards the first cave, anticipating feeling their bodies embrace again. She felt the same way, and followed him into the damp hollow. It was cast in semi darkness as they went further in, and they saw the ground was made up of sand and shingle underfoot. There was a pungent smell of seaweed, which lingered in the air.

Patrick threw his jacket to the ground, hoping this might be comfortable. Elena had other ideas for their love- making. She really did open his eyes to endless possibilities. "Have you read the Karma Sutra?" She whispered while he undressed her.

"No!" He gasped as he felt her exposed breasts in his hands. The urgency he suddenly felt was overwhelming, and he ached to be inside her once again. Elena made him wait as she knelt in front of him, and caressed him tenderly with her mouth.

Patrick was ecstatic, and never in his wildest dreams could he have imagined this sensation. He struggled to control himself as he moaned softly. Elena suddenly got up, and pulled Patrick with her to the far side of the cave. He lifted her effortlessly in his strong arms, and they made love forcefully against the hard rock of the cave wall. Both came together in an erotic passion, they moaned with pleasure panting, and not wanting the feeling to end. The moon rose outside and a filter of light entered the cave. Patrick looked deeply into Elena's eyes. "I love you." He said in a husky tone.

Gently he put her down; and they went and lay together on his jacket. They spoke softly to one another as they wrapped each other in a warm embrace, neither one ready for sleep.

They made love again well into the night, even as the tide crept silently over the floor of the cave. It was only shallow water, which ran up over their entwined bodies, and this only added to their eroticism.

They emerged from the cave at dawn, and heard the far off cry of a seagull as they walked back around the headland holding hands. Exhausted from passion they walked in silence until reaching the foot of the grassy hill. Then Patrick stopped, and turned to face Elena.

"I really do love you." He said intensely as he looked deeply into her eyes. Elena smiled, but didn't say anything in response. Patrick offered to walk her back to her van, but she shook her head saying there was really no need. They kissed again, and then he stood watching as she walked away across the sand. Idly he picked up a piece of driftwood, and drew a heart shape in the sand with the words "Patrick and Elena." in its center. He walked back slowly up the winding path to White Rose Cottage.

Once inside the cottage Patrick felt an overwhelming urge to phone his mother. He wanted to tell her that he had met the girl of his dreams. Patrick stopped suddenly as he slowly repeated out loud. "The girl of my dreams..." Of course he remembered the dream; it had been constant before coming to Ireland. He recalled the dark haired woman from his dream, and he now knew it was Elena without a shadow of doubt. He had been so wrapped up in the euphoric state of his emotions, that he had forgotten the dream until now. Patrick decided not to ring his mother just then, but to keep his secret under wraps for the present time anyway.

He spent the rest of the morning lying in bed, and listening to music in between dozing. It was sometime later in the afternoon, when hearing his mobile ring loudly he awoke abruptly. It was Elena, and she asked him if he wanted to go into the village for a drink later. Patrick agreed, although he really only ever drank the odd glass of wine. It was arranged, and they would meet around nine o'clock that evening.

Meanwhile when Elena had got back to Home farm, she was surprised to see new arrivals. It was the big tour bus, which belonged to the musicians that she had met earlier in Dingle. Dave the lead guitarist was there stroking Pagan as she walked in through the field gate. "Hi." Dave said grinning as Elena approached.

"Well fancy meeting you again." She laughed. He introduced the other members of the group; she nodded a friendly hello. Dave asked if she would like to share breakfast with them. Elena smelt the sizzling bacon, and agreed gratefully. Pagan was thrown a couple of rashers too. She sat with Dave and the others in the luxurious tour bus as they chatted over breakfast. Afterwards she thanked them and offered to wash up, but Dave wouldn't hear of it so she left them to it. When Elena returned to her van she had rung Patrick on her mobile. After their brief conversation she had showered, and now lay down to grab a few hours' kip.

When she awoke Elena took Pagan for a walk along the beach. He had missed her last night as he had been left alone by the van. They spent a couple of hours on the beach, and Pagan ran off all of his energy. Elena decided to walk back along the forest trail, which led back to Home farm. The trail was deserted, and an eerie chilled wind rustled through the tall pine trees. Elena felt sure it was a haunted place, and she quickened her pace; as a shiver ran down her spine. Pagan was up ahead, and when he barked suddenly Elena nearly jumped out her skin with fright. There was a rustle in the undergrowth, and a rabbit hopped out. It scampered across the path, and Elena started laughing, chastising herself for being so timid. They walked on through the tall dark trees, and presently came out onto the roadway, which was opposite Home farm. Elena crossed the road quickly with Pagan at her heels and headed to her van. "Hello dear." Mrs. Ryan waved to her from the courtyard, where she was busy hanging out her washing. Elena waved and called back "hello."

She went into her van leaving Pagan outside because he smelt strongly of briny sea- water. He flopped on the grass contently. Elena noticed there were still a couple of hours to pass before meeting Patrick at the village pub.

She decided to read her Tarot cards to pass the time. She sat at the small table with a large mug of tea. Next she spent a few quiet moments emptying her mind, before taking the cards from the box. Then when she felt relaxed she began to shuffle the deck of cards. She was familiar with the cards, and found them easy to handle. Suddenly she stopped shuffling, sensing the right moment as experienced Tarot readers do. Elena placed the deck face down, and then cut the pack dividing them into three piles. Concentrating again she chose the pile, which she felt drawn to, and moved the others to one side. Elena instantly felt a presence around her as she started to turn the cards over, and she felt a deep sense of sadness shroud her. Elena focused on the cards. Their pictures and symbols spoke to her mind as she received their messages. She felt a warm presence just then right by her shoulder, and she knew it was her late grandmother offering her some comfort.

Elena picked up the cards, and shuffled the whole deck again, before replacing them in the wooden box. Afterwards she made herself a sandwich and some more tea. At that point she switched on her radio, hoping the music would lift her mood. After a while Elena got up, changed her clothes, did her hair and make-up, and left to meet Patrick. She passed by the tour bus, which seemed deserted; as she walked on through the farm gates.

Out on the roadway Elena perceived that there were a few cars about, and they all seemed to be heading in the direction of the village. At that moment a car pulled up slowly beside her. The female driver offered Elena a lift. Elena looked in at the middle - aged woman who posed no real threat, so she accepted her kind offer. She was a friendly type, and chatted pleasantly on their short trip. She pulled up in the village, and parked her small car. Elena thanked her for the lift, and said goodbye as she got out of the car.

The one and only pub was not far away, and Elena soon arrived at the glass doors, which displayed a Happy Hour 5pm to 6pm sign. She pushed the heavy door open, where she was immediately met by gaze of the local clan, who were enjoying their pints of Guinness. They all eyed her suspiciously just for a moment, but Elena walked in bravely. Soon enough they had turned back to their drinks and chat. Elena headed towards the highly polished bar, and she was just about to order a drink when she heard a familiar voice beside her. "Can I buy you a drink?" It was Dave the musician. Elena refused his kind offer shaking her head. Dave seemed disappointed, but she quickly explained that she was meeting a friend here. Elena couldn't see Patrick anywhere as she surveyed the crowded pub. Dave was very persistent with the offer of a drink, which she finally accepted. He asked her to join him, and the other musicians at the table in the corner, at least until whoever she was meeting turned up. She agreed to this as there were not any other free tables, and the pub was surprisingly packed.

Meanwhile Patrick had arrived outside the pub, he felt nervous and extremely agitated. He had never in his life been inside a pub, he and his parents had only frequented hotel bars, which were a bit more refined. He heard the noisy chatter of the crowd within, and the light strains of tin whistle music, which floated in the background. He walked a few paces to a side window, and gazing in he saw Elena sitting with a group of young men. They were all laughing and seemingly enjoying themselves. Instantly Patrick felt a stab of jealousy. Maybe she had forgotten him? She seemed too engrossed in her present company. He felt suddenly stupid and angry with himself .All of his new found confidence rapidly deserted him.

Elena had not forgotten him at all, and she glanced frequently at the large brass clock, which hung above the bar while searching the crowded room for his face. Dave and the other members of the group kept the drinks flowing in a constant stream as well as the conversation. When an hour had passed, and there was still no sign of Patrick, Elena decided to go outside and ring him on her mobile. She rang his number, but there was no reply, and she got his voice mail service instead so she left a short message.

After another hour had passed, Dave and his friends decided to drive down to Kinvarra, which was the nearest town to Doorus. They wanted to see what the night- life there had to offer.

"Do you want to come?" Dave asked Elena.

"Oh I don't know." She answered undecidedly.

"You might as well; your friend hasn't shown up!" Dave remarked casually.

"Yes okay." She felt reluctant, but Patrick hadn't shown up, and she wondered if he was ok. They got into the tour bus, and Elena decided to ring Patrick, once more. Again she got the voice mail, so she left another message. She sat beside Eddie, who was a large burley man with tattoos covering his arms. He was the delegated driver as he had the least to drink out of the group. He promised to go onto soft drinks, for the remainder of the evening. The tour bus pulled away, and they all waved goodbye to Doorus and its only pub.

Meanwhile Patrick had walked back along the country lane to the cottage. He had gone inside briefly and casually thrown his jacket onto his bed. He was just about to go out through the back door, when his mobile phone rang shrilly. He went back into the bedroom, and retrieved the phone from his jacket pocket. "Hello mother." Patrick said deflated.

"No, nothing's wrong, I'm just a little tired." He lied. This didn't deter his mother from diving headlong into a full blown account of her usual conversation. Patrick held the phone away from his ear, and then every few minutes he brought the receiver to his mouth to utter. "Yes mother." After an hour passed by, and his hand ached she finally said goodbye and hung up. Patrick dropped the phone onto the bed with a sigh of relief. He walked out through the back door of the cottage.

The night was cooler this evening, and darkness shrouded the air veiling the moon and stars. A cold breeze blew across the bay, gusting sharply at Patrick's light cotton shirt. He shivered involuntary, and suddenly felt very lonely. He decided to take a slow walk along the deserted beach, hoping to dispel his dark mood. He passed through the little wooden gate at the end of the garden, and headed down the sandy track. When he reached the beach below, he didn't bother to take his shoes off. Instead he just started to walk slowly with his shoulders hunched forward, and his head hung low. The sea was mysteriously dark and restless, and it seemed to match his mood. The waves heaved forward ferociously as they crashed callously against the rocky headland. Their white spray splashed onto the cool, grey jagged rock. Patrick stood alone watching the motion of the sea as dark thoughts clouded his mind. And just for a split second he thought seriously of just walking into the sea and disappearing forever. Suddenly the wind whispered lightly, and he thought or imagined he had heard Elena's voice calling his name. He turned around quickly; looking for her and his eyes scanned the deserted beach as he strained to see through the veil of darkness.

The large rocks around the bay loomed in the darkness, casting shadows across the wet sand as Patrick walked towards them. Elena wasn't there, and he sighed heavily realizing that he must have imagined her calling him. Digging his hands deeply into his trouser pockets, he ascended the sandy track slowly. Back up the hill and through the garden, he entered the cottage. There Patrick went straight to bed, and soon sleep overcame his weary mind.

Elena, Dave and the group had spent a lively evening in Kinvarra. They had gone from one end of the main street to the other sampling the local beer, and enjoying the entertainment. Elena had casually fought off Dave's romantic attempts as he tried to get her alone. He took her refusals light heartedly, although he promised seriously that he wouldn't give up. Last orders were called at the pub; where they took another drink for good measure. This concluded when all were finally satiated. They called it a night, and reluctantly trooped back onto the tour bus. They were all laughing, and in high spirits as they started out on the return journey to Doorus. Their mood was still lively as Eddie led the group in a hearty sing-song. They travelled along the winding country roads at the dead of night.

Patrick woke suddenly from his restless sleep. Beads of perspiration trickled down his forehead, and his body clammy with sweat. Something is terribly wrong were his first thoughts as a sick stomach churning feeling overcame him. He looked at the bedside clock which showed two thirty am. He got up and walked to the window where gazed out into a black void. He lifted the tiny latch and pushed the window open, instantly smelling the familiar fragrance of the roses, which rambled up the cottage wall. "Elena." He whispered softly into the cool night air.

Just then he heard a loud rap at the front door. Patrick rushed straight to the door, and opened it quickly sensing the urgency. "Mr. Ryan?" Patrick asked surprised to find the older man standing on the doorstep. Mr. Ryan's eyes looked a little larger than usual and his complexion was ashen grey. He spoke quickly and matter-of-factly although managing to keep his tone low. "There's been an accident a mile out from Doorus, Mrs. Ryan said I was to come and fetch you straight away. You must come to Home farm, right away." He spoke calmly while looking directly into Patrick's eyes.

Patrick immediately went into an automatic mode, where the senses become protectively dull. And the body reacts as if in slow motion. He picked up his jacket from the bed, and followed Mr. Ryan out of the house towards his waiting car. Once seated in the car Patrick heard his own voice echo as if from a distance as he asked. "What kind of accident?"

"Mrs. Ryan will explain when we get there." Mr. Ryan answered in a low voice. Patrick suddenly thought this could just be a weird dream, and he might wake up soon.

In a short time they had reached Home farm, where all of the lights were on in the house. Patrick followed Mr. Ryan into the well- lit kitchen. There he was immediately given a large glass of brandy, and told to sit down. He sat at the large pine breakfast table, facing Mrs. Ryan who also had a glass in her hand.

She quickly swigged down the last few drops of her brandy. Slowly she placed the glass down and then looked up at him. Tears welled in her bright blue eyes, and she sniffed loudly before attempting to speak. "There's been an accident." She repeated Mr. Ryan's words, and then waited for some reaction. Patrick's eyes turned from deep blue to a misty grey, and he stared straight ahead of him. She knew he had heard, and she took his hand in her own trembling hand. She squeezed it tightly. Suddenly she saw tears well up in his eyes, and roll slowly down his face. She knew that he had guessed, but she continued to speak gently and calmly. Mr. Ryan poured himself a brandy and joined them at the table.

"The tour bus collided with a heavy goods lorry on the coastal road." Mrs. Ryan sniffed again, and tried to contain her tears as she spoke. There was a long pause as she waited for Patrick to speak, but he didn't. The agonizing silence seemed eternal. Mrs. Ryan couldn't contain her tears any longer, they were choking her, and so she let them fall softly and quietly.

Mr. Ryan spoke up then. "The bus went off the road and the lorry was forced into the side of the hill." He too then paused, giving Patrick a chance to take in the information. Patrick sat still unmoved and stared at the wall ahead. He heard Mrs. Ryan's soft sobs beside him and Mr. Ryan's deep sigh. Somewhere deep down inside of himself, he hoped that this really was just a bad dream, and that he would wake up soon. The minutes ticked away, and the silence was deathly still, but he could feel Mrs. Ryan's trembling hand holding his own.

Patrick forced the words out of his mouth as he whispered. "Is Elena okay?" His words hung in the air suspended, and he knew the answer. Deep within his chest a sharp pain stabbed him, piercing straight through his heart. It broke instantly, into a thousand agonizing shards.

"There were no survivors, they were all killed." Mr. Ryan gulped as he relayed the terrible news, and a lump stuck in his throat. He shook his head and sighed.

Patrick was aware of being led upstairs to one of their spare bedrooms, and being made to lie down. His body did this automatically; he lay with glazed eyes staring up at the bedroom ceiling. He listened to his own shallow breathing; it seemed to echo in his numb mind. All of a sudden from outside, a dog howled loudly, its sad haunting cry as it mourned the loss of its beloved owner.

Chapter Nine

In the few days which had passed since Elena's death, Patrick's mother had immediately flown to Ireland after receiving Mrs. Ryan's phone call. Patrick was in a terrible state, and his mother returned with him to England on the next available flight. Mrs. Ryan had said that she would inform him of any funeral arrangements as soon as she had met with Elena's brother. She had spoken to Patrick softly, hoping he was listening to her, but by his glazed expression she couldn't be sure.

When they arrived back at the family home Patrick went straight to his apartment, and shut himself away. His mother was very concerned; she sent a maid over with a dinner tray of hot soup and freshly baked rolls. When the maid returned without the tray she felt relieved, at least he was going to eat something. She discussed the situation with her husband; they both agreed that he would need a little time before they sent him back to Medical school.

It was much later in the evening when Patrick picked up his mobile phone. He was going to ring Mrs. Ryan although he wasn't sure what he wanted to say. Just then he noticed the message box flashing on his phone. Pressing the access buttons he held the phone to his ear, and listened. There were two messages, which Elena had left on the night of the accident. Patrick turned as white as a ghost as he listened to her beautiful voice. He replayed the messages immediately, and pressed the phone closer to his ear. A sharp pain stabbed at his chest, and he gasped loudly just before the tears began to stream down his cheeks. Patrick wiped them away quickly with the back of his hand, and he sniffed hard. He refused to believe that she had gone.

Just then he heard a loud knock at his apartment door, and he got up to answer it leaving the phone on the chair. Patrick opened the door slightly ajar, he saw his mother's shadowy face eagerly waiting to be let in. Patrick remained in the doorway blocking her entrance; he didn't want her to come in. He didn't want to talk to her either, but she stood there for a few moments. She handed him a bag of clothes. "It's your clean washing; I had the maid see to it for you dear." She spoke dejectedly.

"Thank you." Patrick replied quietly, and took the bag from her. He closed the door, and left her on the doorstep. He walked absently into his bedroom, and dropped the bag of clothes onto the floor. The room suddenly felt stiflingly warm, and Patrick opened a window. He lay down on top of his large deluxe king size bed. How different it seemed compared to the old- fashioned brass bed, which he had slept in at the cottage. He closed his eyes, and began to let his mind wander through his recent memories. He felt the warm evening breeze softly blowing in through the window. Patrick turned his face towards the window, and he suddenly felt something hard just under the pillow. He reached under the pillow to find out what it was, and his hand felt the mobile phone. Slightly startled Patrick grabbed the phone and sat up quickly. How did it get there? He was puzzled as he remembered leaving it on the chair in the lounge. He sighed loudly as he put it on the pillow next to him, and lay down again closing his tired eyes. What did it really matter how the phone had got there? He thought to himself.

Patrick slept restlessly that night; he dreamt he was back in Ireland, where he had just met Elena for the first time on the beach. He smiled as he saw her emerging from the sea, clad in her skimpy bikini, which showed her curvaceous tanned body. The dream leapt forward to the picnic scene, where they were laughing together, and drinking wine blissfully happy. He sighed deeply in his dream like state. He could smell the salty sea air, and he watched the waves gently lap against the soft golden sand. This was the happiest he had ever been in his entire life as the memories replayed through his subconscious. Patrick woke up suddenly, he felt disorientated momentarily, and then he slowly realized that he was back at home in England. It was still dark outside, and a deep remorseful sadness washed over him instantaneously as he recalled fragments of the dream.

He felt lonely and miserable in the empty king-size bed, and he just lay there looking into the darkness. The only glimmer of light came from the mobile phone beside him on the pillow. He played Elena's messages again, and lay back listening. Her soft sexy voice spoke to him in the dark shrouded room. "I'm here waiting for you, where are you Patrick?"
He held the phone beside his face, and closed his eyes while her words floated in the air echoing in his mind.

The next morning he received a phone call from Elena's brother. He spoke to Patrick briefly telling him that Mrs. Ryan had given him the phone number. The arrangements had been made to fly Elena's body home. The funeral would be held on Friday at two o'clock. Details were then given to Patrick of the church and the location. Patrick scribbled down the information on a notepad quickly, and then said thank you. He confirmed that he would attend the funeral.

Patrick wandered around in a semi state of undress for the rest of the day. He didn't really know what to do. The only funeral he had ever attended was his grandmothers. She was elderly; it hadn't been a great shock when she had passed away peacefully. This felt so different; he had only known Elena for a short time, but he felt sure that it was real love. It was only a week ago that she was alive; and they had made love on the beach. Life seemed so cruel and unfair to him, and he just didn't want to believe that she had gone so suddenly out of his life.

His mother called again at his apartment and she had looked a little disturbed when he opened the door, and she saw his unshaven gaunt appearance. This time she was determined to get in through the front door. She pushed past him forcefully to gain entry.

"Oh dear we can't leave those there." She remarked, noticing the bag of clothes on the bedroom floor. "I'll send the maid over to sort this out, and clean up a little." She spoke rapidly as she surveyed the bedroom. She saw the scribbled note. "Oh is that the arrangements for your friend's funeral?" She asked, knowing full well that it was.

"Yes." Patrick snapped sharply, he knew that his mother had the eyes of a hawk. "Her name is Elena and she was more than just a friend." He stated in an aggressive tone.

"Oh yes dear I understand." She soothed, and then she sighed as she continued. "I can attend the funeral with you, but I'm not sure whether your father, will be available to. He's such a busy man as you know." She waited patiently fully aware that her son was only vaguely listening. She sat down on the large leather sofa, wanting to just be there for him.

Her company seemed unnecessary and quite suffocating to Patrick. He quickly dressed in his bedroom before walking straight passed her, and out into the gardens.

Outside the air was still and quiet, Patrick stood for a moment breathing in the cool, crisp, clear air. He looked over to the huge oak tree at the far side of the sweeping lawn, which had stood there for what seemed like an eternity. Its large leafy branches implied a serene sanctuary, which called to the spirit of his inner child.

He walked towards the tree across the dewy grass, recalling from his shy painful childhood that this had been his comfort zone. He remembered the many hours he had spent hiding in the great oak's welcoming branches. His hands reached towards the hard gnarled thick trunk. Patrick stood momentarily feeling the intricacy of the patterned bark, which had been woven and shaped over many years. Just then he grabbed a lower branch, and quickly pulled his body upwards. Patrick easily swung his long legs up onto the outstretched lower branch. He knew that he was now concealed from the harsh outside world, and his mother.

Patrick felt overwhelmed up there nestling in the security of the oak's great branches. He felt a sharp stabbing pain in his chest, and he gulped hard before the tears burst from his eyes. His whole body shook uncontrollably, wracked with pain and sorrow. He sobbed and then gasped as he struggled to breathe. He felt a strong urge come over him, and he wanted to bang his head against the hard surface of the tree. Patrick thought quite irrationally that this would somehow ease his pain, and take it all away in one blow. Suddenly he felt something touch his shoulder, slightly and ever so lightly. Patrick didn't lift his head immediately, and he kept his eyes shut. He froze momentarily and his tears seemed to stop mid flow. He opened his eyes slowly, but there was no one visible beside him on the large branch although he felt as if someone were there. Had he imagined the touch on his shoulder? It had been so slight, but it had felt real. Patrick looked around through the large leafy branches, and he breathed in deeply.

A few strands of sunlight crept in through the dense tree, and sent shards of hazy light beams dancing through the air. A gentle breeze rustled through the leaves, and Patrick thought he heard someone speak whispering on the light breeze. He heard his name called, and he looked around feeling quite bewildered. He felt certain he had heard his name called, but again there wasn't anybody there.

Patrick eased himself down slowly from his comfort zone, and out from the sanctuary of the old tree. His head swam with nausea, and he felt tired as he walked back across the lawn to his apartment. The maid was just leaving as he entered the apartment, but Patrick didn't acknowledge her presence. She was a young quiet girl, and she smiled politely as they passed each other. Patrick just looked through her, and walked directly to his bedroom where he closed the door, and turned the key sharply.   The next day he spent alone behind the closed door, ignoring his mother's attempts to cajole him. Three trays of food were brought to his door, but were later taken away completely untouched.

Finally it was Friday, and the day of Elena's funeral. Patrick sat beside his mother in the chauffeur driven black Bentley. On the back window shelf, there was a huge bouquet of white Lilies, which were chosen by his mother. She imagined she was helping to take the strain off her son. Patrick barely glanced at the flowers; he had not made a single comment in reply to his mother's persistent idle chatter. She looked carefully at her son's vacant expression, and then she sighed turning her gaze to the car window. She placed her impeccably manicured, white gloved hand onto his stone cold unresponsive hand. She recalled the intense conversation, which she had with her husband the previous evening. Patrick's father had informed her that they would let him get the funeral over with, and then things would return to normal. In reality things had never been normal for Patrick, not until he had gone to Ireland, and met Elena. Sadly his parents had no conception of their son's real needs.

His mother felt that she was doing her duty, by just being there to support her son today. The day was dismal grey and overcast. Ironically it seemed fitting for the daunting occasion. The Bentley pulled into the small church yard car park. A small crowd had gathered there, and they each turned and stared. Patrick had no idea who the people were, he felt suddenly like an intruder. Elena had spoken so little of her family. Patrick had no idea that her mother had died previously, and her father had left her when she was a child. He looked awkwardly at the small gathering of blank faces, which stood huddled together under a mass of black umbrellas.

Patrick stood with his mother awkwardly outside the small chapel. He looked around, and then he saw two familiar faces, which appeared quite unexpectedly from behind the crowd. Patrick breathed a huge sigh of relief as Mr. and Mrs. Ryan approached him. Mrs. Ryan greeted Patrick, and hugged him affectionately. She whispered a few comforting words to him, while she tried to conceal the pity she felt; he seemed such a lonely young man. She was one of the very few people who knew of his love for Elena. Mr. and Mrs. Ryan had only met Elena briefly, but they had decided to come to the funeral and pay their respects.

The crowd who were making small talk suddenly fell silent as the funeral hearse arrived. Patrick felt numb as he watched the long black car halt, by the open church doorway where a priest stood waiting for them. The undertakers lifted the highly polished wooden coffin, and carried it into the dimly lit church. A dark haired man followed the procession.

"That's her brother." Mrs. Ryan whispered as she linked Patrick's arm, and led him gently towards the church doors. His legs felt like lead weight, and he moved in slow motion with the others entering the church. He focused only on the wooden box, which moved slowly and reverently ahead of him. The massive bouquet of Lilies and red Roses, which were strewn on top of the coffin were suddenly just a blur. Patrick felt as if he were going to pass out. Suddenly a strong arm supported him; and he turned gratefully to see Mr. Ryan beside him, guiding him towards a dark wooden pew. There he welcomed the added support, of the wooden frame to lean on. The comfort of the Ryan's beside him, he knew he would always remember.

They heard music playing from a depressingly somber organ. A priest issued his sermon, and his words resonated with the cold stone walls. Patrick focused on the coffin, which was standing alone by the marble alter. In his mind he refused to believe, that the woman he loved lay dead in that box. No he didn't want to believe it, so instead he convinced his muddled mind that none of this was real.

A loud buzzing noise suddenly pierced the air. The congregation turned in unison to see where the noise had come from. Patrick gasped; mortified as he realized it was his mobile phone buzzing in his over coat pocket. "I'm terribly sorry!" He said loudly as he moved quickly from his seat, and rushed from the church. Outside he took a deep breath, God how awful! He thought aloud, feeling a hot flush of embarrassment; creep up around his neck. He quickly felt for the phone in his pocket, and he walked away across the church yard. The message indicator flashed on his phone, and Patrick wondered who an earth had sent him a message. He pressed the screen, and held the phone to his ear listening as he walked along the gravel path, flanked either side by headstones. Just then he heard Elena's message play clearly. He didn't quite understand why the phone had buzzed, when there clearly wasn't a new message. Maybe the phone was faulty he wondered, but how ironic was the timing of Elena's message.

Patrick felt a strange sensation pass over him, could it be her spirit was here with him today. It all seemed weird, and a little daunting. He had no idea of whether he believed in ghosts or spirits. He hadn't any cause to think about these things before, and he felt unsure of what his beliefs were. Patrick followed the path which led around to the rear of the small stone church. He felt quite uneasy, but eventually he came to an undisturbed corner of the grave- yard. A huge Lime tree obscured the sky from this corner, and the air seemed to stand still in this quiet spot. Patrick took refuge under the large leafy branches, where he listened once more to Elena's last message. Her voice sounded so full of life as if she was standing right beside him, and he shivered involuntarily.

"There you are!" Someone spoke suddenly and Patrick leapt out of his skin.

"Mother you startled me." He said alarmed as his heart pounded in his chest.

"I've been looking for you everywhere; I thought you had gone without me." His mother explained anxiously. Subsequently she told him that "the funeral was over. He had missed the coffin being lowered into the grave. All the sympathizers had gone to the local hall, where refreshments were being served. I don't think we need attend that dear, maybe we should go home now." She announced finally stopping to draw breath.

Patrick nodded in agreement as they walked back to their car. They drove home leaving the dismal little grey stone church behind.

Thank God that's over! His mother thought feeling silently relieved.

A whole week passed by before Patrick returned to the grave- yard. This time he went alone one morning quite early, he carried a bouquet of large white roses. He found her grave easily recognizable by the freshly dug mound of earth. There was a small simple wooden cross, which stood with her name on it. He placed the bouquet of roses beside the cross. The card attached to the flowers read, for you my only true love. Patrick turned and walked away because now, more than ever, he felt sure her spirit did not rest there.

Chapter Ten

Weeks passed by and Patrick knew his parents were waiting for him to announce his return to Medical school. His mother persistently invited him up to the house for dinner, but he repeatedly thwarted her invitations. He had tried to make an effort in his appearance, and had discarded the unshaven look. His parents hoped that he was going to become his old self again. Most of the days he spent away from home; he visited the library, art galleries and even the local leisure center. He went anywhere just to escape his mother, and to keep his mind active. Each evening Patrick returned to a lonely life, and an empty apartment.

One such evening he had returned home, to find a hand written note in his mail- box. It was from his mother announcing she was holding a dinner party in honor of his birthday, which was the following evening. "God, is it my birthday?" Patrick remarked. He checked the date on his phone, and he realized it was his birthday tomorrow!

So there was no avoiding this he thought, and surely she would have gone to a lot of unnecessary trouble. He decided to take a shower, and not think about the birthday until tomorrow. During the recent days Patrick had begun to cope, and he managed to occupy his time. The evenings were when he felt the loneliest. He had slept restlessly ever since Elena's death, and had recurring dreams of the times they had spent together. In reality he was barely existing, not living or leading the life he could have. Patrick didn't want the dreams to stop because they and his mobile phone were all that he had left of Elena. In his restless sleep at least he was loved and happy, but in reality his life was empty.

There had been a couple of strange incidents during the past few weeks, but Patrick had not been able to make sense of them. The first occurred when he had been sitting alone one evening, and his C.D player had started to play a song, which he hadn't programmed it to do. It had startled him when he heard the music start, and then he became angry banging the C.D with his fist. It had broken in many pieces, so he had thrown it away. Patrick had gone to bed thinking it must be faulty. A couple of days later when he had been feeling depressed, he felt sure someone had kissed his neck. There in his apartment he had actually felt lips caress his neck. Startled again he had jumped up, but he couldn't see anybody there.

He convinced himself that he must be imagining things, or else in danger of losing his sanity!

This evening as he undressed in his en-suite bathroom, and turned on the shower he heard his name whispered in the steamy air. It was Elena's voice he felt certain, but then it faded away. All he could hear was the gushing spray of water from the shower. Oh God how he missed her! Patrick wished with all his heart that she was here with him making love to him in the shower. Suddenly in his mind she was there beside him. Their bodies were entwined together naked, under the powerful splashing water. She was smiling as she kissed, and caressed the whole length of his lithe body. He felt happy with the warm, sensual wetness, of her naked skin next to his. The love- making was passionate and erotic, both reached climax wildly. Patrick sighed deeply as he opened his eyes knowing she had gone. The warm water splashed onto his face, and he reached forward and turned off the steamy shower. He put on a warm, luxurious toweling robe, and he went to his bedroom to lie down. Patrick slept contentedly for the first time since Elena's death.

It was early the next morning when he heard his mother's familiar voice; she called to him through the letter- box. Patrick sprang from his bed, and rushed to open the door. His vibrant expression and smiling face quite startled his mother at first. "Did you sleep well, dear?" She carried in his birthday breakfast tray, and eyed him warily. She was surprised to see an overnight transformation in her grieving son. "Happy Birthday." She handed him a couple of cards, which he accepted gratefully. One was from his parents, and the other card was from cook. She always sent him a card each birthday and Christmas. Patrick had never received more than two cards on any birthday, which he could remember.

He opened them, and said thank you as he stood them up on the marble mantle shelf, either side of his Louis XIV ornate gold clock. His mother kissed him lightly on his cheek. After which she reminded him of the time, which he would be expected to attend the huge birthday ball. She was pleased that at least he seemed keen on the idea. It made her happy to see a certain sparkle, return to his eyes. She got up to leave, and ever so slightly moved her birthday card forward on the shelf, giving it a more prominent position than cooks.

Patrick went out after breakfast deciding to go into town, and buy some new music, a shirt perhaps and maybe shoes. He carried his mobile in his pocket, alongside his credit card. He sped off along the gravel drive in his black B.M.W. Twenty minutes later he was parked, and walking casually along the main high street. The town was made up of modern designer shops, and smart restaurants and exclusive boutiques. There was also a large Mall, which housed all the familiar retail outlets, and Patrick headed for this first. He spent a long time in the music shop, and spent a good deal of money. He purchased ten C.D's, and at least seven D.V.D's. He decided to upgrade his music system too. Paying with his credit card he signed the receipt, and left the delivery address.

Next he went into his favorite footwear boutique. He bought a few pairs of shoes, and a couple of pairs of the most expensive sports shoes. The staff there knew Patrick well. They were over friendly to their most important customer; in fact they verged on the edge of creepiness to accommodate his every need. Patrick paid with plastic once more and left carrying the large exclusive paper bags, which contained the shoes.

He felt a little weighed down so he decided to head back to his car and off load the bags. Patrick turned down a side road, which was a shorter way to his car. He was startled as his mobile phone vibrated in his jacket pocket. He stopped, and at first struggled to get to it with his hands full.

Just then a voice spoke from behind him. "Here let me hold those for you." A young woman came around in front of him.

Patrick looked surprised and then smiled shyly. "Thank you." He said handing the bags to her. "If you are sure you don't mind." He added clumsily.

He pulled out the mobile, and saw the message indicator was flashing. Patrick touched the screen and listened to Elena's familiar voice. He shut the phone off.

"Are you okay?" The woman asked.

Patrick had gone a little pale, but recovered himself quickly. "I'm okay."

"You don't look it." The woman persisted. "Why don't you come into my shop for a minute, and sit down?" She took his arm and led him into the nearby shop. Patrick sat on a wooden chair, which she pulled out from behind a glass counter. She put his bags beside him. "I'll get you a drink of water." She disappeared through a beaded curtain.

Patrick waited patiently, and glanced around the strange little shop. He noticed the dress rails of assorted unfashionable clothes. He sniffed noticing a strange smell which came from the clothes. His nose wrinkled slightly, and he wondered why anyone would try to sell, these things. The beaded curtain jingled as the woman came through carrying a chipped grey mug, which she handed politely to him. "Sorry but they're all chipped!" She announced noticing his distasteful expression.

"That's okay thank you." Patrick took the mug and sipped politely. He looked at the woman properly for the first time since their encounter. He noticed she was very pretty, and had beautiful dark brown eyes. She blushed slightly as he stared at her. Patrick spoke quickly turning his gaze around the shop.

He was amazed when she told him that it was in fact a Charity shop. "All the proceeds go to Africa, and Asia to provide much needed medical supplies."

"Do they really?" Patrick was suddenly intrigued. "And people actually buy these clothes?" He asked.

She informed him that they relied on public donations. "Oh I see." Patrick said fumbling in his jacket pocket, to find his wallet.

"No, no, I didn't mean you to come in here, and make a donation." The woman laughed a little embarrassed. Patrick smiled awkwardly, and then announced. "It's my birthday today that's why I bought all these." He said glancing at the designer bags, containing his expensive footwear. It was his turn to feel a little embarrassed now.

"I'm Helena." She proffered her hand in a friendly gesture.

"Patrick." He replied taking her hand. He smiled pleasantly, and then another little awkward silence followed.

"I really should be going now." Patrick handed her the grey chipped mug. He retrieved his bags, and headed towards the door.

"Happy birthday Patrick" Elena said lightly. He smiled, and went out through the door.

Patrick made his way to the car park as large droplets of rain began to fall. The sky had changed becoming dark, and overcast. A storm was threatening. Patrick dropped the bags onto the back seat, suddenly feeling a gust of wind blow around him. He heard a soft whisper. "Helena...Elena..." on the breeze. He shivered and got into the driving seat quickly. Had he imagined the whisper? He thought of the pretty faced Helena, but then memories of Elena flooded his mind. His thoughts were cleared suddenly by a loud hoot, and an infuriated driver. Patrick realized that he had been holding up the traffic at a green light. He concentrated on his driving, and soon arrived back at home. The huge iron gates, which stood between great stone piers pretentiously, formed the entrance. Patrick drove up the half mile driveway, turning to the left of the stone fountain, and to the private road that led off to his apartment. Home, sweet home! He sighed as his mood became unexpectedly cool.

Chapter Eleven

At quarter to eight that evening, Patrick had showered, and was now wearing a deep blue, luxurious Egyptian toweling robe. He stood in his walk in dressing room, and surveyed the rows of meticulously neat designer clothes. There were racks upon racks of shoes. His mind did a flash back to the charity shop, which he had unusually encountered that day. Patrick thought that surely medical supplies can't be funded properly by old clothes. He thought of Helena, and he smiled as he remembered the grey chipped mug.

At eight fifteen precisely Patrick entered his parent's mansion, dressed impeccably in black dinner suit, white tuxedo and black tie. His mother was impressed as he knew she would be, and she kissed his cheek lightly. His father also dressed in the same attire walked slowly towards him, carrying a large crystal brandy glass already near depleted.

"Happy Birthday Patrick!" He boomed forcing a smile, and shaking Patrick's hand in a cold fish manner.

His parents as usual had spared no expense for the birthday ball. What would their high class friends, and neighbor's think if they had stinted on their only son, and heirs birthday bash.

Patrick noticed the string orchestra set on a podium, at the far side of the room. The line of waiters armed with silver trays, and champagne filled glasses waiting for his mother's well timed cue. The enormous white silk clothed tables, which were set along the entire length of the wall with an array of fine delicacies, which the caterers had arranged. An enormous fresh watered salmon mousse, lay complete with its head, and tail on a large silver platter. The salmon's lifeless eye was staring up at the antique crystal chandelier. A spit- roasted pig, complete with red shiny apple in its mouth lay on another platter.

"Do you like it darling, does it meet with your approval?" His mother followed his gaze around the room. Patrick knew this was a statement, which she had made rather than a question.

He smiled turning towards his mother. "Thank you mother, it really is splendid." He said graciously. His mother smiled as he knew she would. His father clicked his fingers towards a waiter demanding he get him a refill.

Guests arrived in their grandeur and finery. The room was lit up by the clash of the crystal chandelier droplets, which reflected the precious stone rings, bracelets, and necklaces worn by the female guests. Each male guest wore a black dinner suit with a white tuxedo, and black tie. Looking like a troop of over grown penguins. Patrick stood beside his parents, welcoming his guests as they arrived. He felt a little nauseated after he had shook the hundred, and fiftieth guest's hand. He wondered how many his mother had actually invited.

His mind began to drift along with the light classical music, which was played by the string orchestra. Just then Patrick felt a slight pat on his arm, and was bought out of the trance.

"Lady Isabella Imogen Stubbs." The usher announced as a tall, blond, slender woman entered the room. She had a thin, tight lipped pursed mouth, which turned neither up nor down at the corners. Her eyes were cold blue, and seemed like glass marbles set in her porcelain doll type face. She stood directly in front of Patrick, and proffered her white gloved hand towards him. He touched it lightly, and then saw his mother's eyes suddenly light up as she patted his father's arm. Lady Isabella escorted by her own parents moved into the ballroom. They thankfully were the last guests to arrive.

The evening went boringly well, waltzes were danced and toasts were made. All of the guests had their fill of fine wine and food. Patrick began to have an uneasy feeling that his mother was playing at match-maker. He soon realized that Lady Isabella was the only single, unattached female guest of his own age. His mother constantly coaxed them to dance together. She declared he would have to be a gentleman, and escort Isabella for the rest of the evening!

Isabella was cool and stand- offish for the most part of the evening. Her father took her aside and had a quiet word with her. Then quite unexpectedly the ice-maiden melted, and strangely warmed to Patrick. She even managed to crack her tight- lipped mouth, into a forced smile. Patrick was puzzled, but acted accordingly as the politeness of society required. It was in the early hours of the morning, when most of the guests had begun to trail off and leave. Isabella had feigned a little exhaustion, and politely asked Patrick to take her out onto the balcony for a breath of fresh air. He led her outside not noticing his mother's contented look from the far side of the room.

Patrick leaned against the stone pillared wall, and steadied himself. The cool breeze mingled with the large amount of alcohol he had consumed, and he felt light headed. Isabella took a step towards him, and shivered in an exaggerated fashion. "It's cold out here." She simpered.

"Shall we go back inside?" Patrick asked.

"No." She whispered moving closer to him. He looked at her wondering what had she meant, but he was a little too inebriated to respond.

"Hold me." She commanded as she pushed her long, willowy body against him. She lifted his arms around her.

"Oh." Patrick just managed to utter before her mouth pounced on his face, and she kissed him willfully. Suddenly there was a loud crash as a huge terracotta urn fell from the balcony above. It smashed into sharp fragments, and just missed Lady Isabella by inches as it hit the stone flags. She screamed, and instantly released Patrick. She fled back into the ballroom. Some of the guests came out to see what had caused the commotion. They were shocked to see the huge urn lying in pieces, amongst a heap of compost and Ivy. Patrick stood motionless only inches away.

"Oh my dear son, are you hurt darling?" His mother exclaimed rushing to him.

"I'm fine mother really." He answered slowly, and he looked up to the balcony above wondering how on earth that urn had fallen. He felt puzzled as to why it had happened at that precise moment. They all returned to the ballroom, where now only a few guests remained. The orchestra was busy packing away their instruments. Lady Isabella overcome with shock was being escorted by her parents, out to their waiting chauffeured car. In her mind she felt certain the falling urn had been meant to fall on her. Somehow her parents matchmaking plan had been sabotaged, but by who? Her mother sat beside her shaken somewhat, while her father ranted, and raged as though the whole incident had been her fault!

"Have you any idea how much debt we are in? We are facing the embarrassment of bankruptcy? We stand to lose everything unless you marry that filthy rich, young Patrick!" Her father stressed raising his voice considerably.

"Please dear not in front of the driver!" His wife pleaded. They drove home in complete silence, and only the muffled sobs of Lady Isabella were heard.

Meanwhile Patrick thanked his parents for the party, and he left then to go home. Back in his plush apartment he undressed down to his black silk, boxer shorts, and lay sprawled lazily on top of his king size bed. The alcohol had made him a little dizzy, and his head began to swim with thoughts of the evening's events. The tall willowy figure of Lady Isabella popped into his head. Just then remarkably the spit roasted pigs head appeared in place of her face. Patrick giggled she did look strange, and then she disappeared. Next the image of the fallen urn took her place. Patrick lay there wondering momentarily how on earth it had fallen. Another image came to him quite suddenly. It was Elena and she was bikini clad, and walking out of the sea….

Oh how beautiful she looked Patrick sighed deeply, and holding that image in his mind he drifted slowly off into a deep sleep. He heard the gentle lapping of the waves running up the beach in his mind as the distant memories soothed him to sleep.

The next morning at breakfast Patrick recalled he'd had the strangest dream. He had been dressed in a safari suit, and traveling in a khaki jeep over the rugged terrain of Africa; at least he thought it had been Africa. There were lions in the bush and antelopes springing around. What on earth he was doing there he had no idea, but with him was Helena the girl from the charity shop. She was actually driving the jeep, and also wearing safari dress. It was bizarre, but he couldn't remember why they were there.

After breakfast he showered and dressed. He stood in his familiar walk in wardrobe when a sudden thought struck him. Patrick gazed at row upon row of expensive clothing, and then he picked out a handful of designer shirts, and a few pairs of very expensive shoes. He found a large hold -all and put all the items in it, he grabbed his car keys and carried the bag out to his B.M.W.

Patrick arrived in town, and parked his car. He carried the loaded bag, and headed down the side

street to the Charity shop. As he pushed the faded red painted door, a little bell rang above his head. Patrick stood in the middle of the shop, and waited for Helena to appear. He got quite a surprise when an old grey haired woman emerged from the beaded curtain.
"Hello, can I help you?" She asked in a friendly tone.

Patrick faltered for a moment, and just smiled politely. He offered the hold-all towards her.
"Oh a donation is it?" She inquired gratefully taking the bag. Patrick nodded and stood still waiting.
"Thank you very much." The woman smiled again. Patrick still didn't move.
"Oh I'm sorry dear, did you want the bag back?"
"No not at all." Patrick replied. Instantly a rush of courage overcame him. "Actually I came to see Helena is she here?"

A twinkle passed over the old woman's eyes. "Yes Helena's just popped out for her break; she should be back in five minutes or so."

"Okay, I'll wait." Patrick replied eagerly, and he felt a surge of excitement. The old woman got excited too, when she opened the hold-all. "Oh my word, I've never seen such beautiful clothes, how kind of you." Patrick blushed, and he hoped they would be useful as saleable items. The woman started to hang, and price them straight -away; they rarely had such quality items donated.

A few minutes passed by before Helena entered carrying a large brown paper bag. "Hello." She spoke seemingly pleased to see Patrick.

"Hello Helena." Patrick replied, and then blushed slightly. She seemed impressed that he had remembered her name. When she learned from the older woman that Patrick had given all the fabulous clothes; she was overwhelmed by his generosity. Patrick actually ended up staying the whole afternoon in the shop. He helped the two women to change the shabby window display, to one which was far more appealing. By the end of the afternoon they had made a few substantial sales. Furthermore he and Helena had become quite well acquainted with one another. Eventually Patrick invited her out for a meal. He was pleased when she agreed. He took details of her address, and also made a mental note to bring in a decent tea set when he next visited.

Chapter Twelve

They met later that evening at eight, when Patrick arrived in his shiny black B.M.W outside her small terraced house. Helena wore a simple black dress with stockings and stilettos, which showed off her shapely legs. Patrick got quite excited as she edged slowly into the front seat of his car, and he got a glimpse of her thigh. He revved up the engine and drove off towards the town. He had booked a table for eight thirty at the best Italian restaurant, which was called Antonio's.

They sat opposite each other in a romantic candlelit alcove, and sipped fine wine. Helena's eyes sparkled, reflecting attractively in the candle light. Patrick commented how on beautiful she looked. She smiled pleasantly, and started to talk about her work. She told him how eager she was to go out to the disaster regions abroad and how she wanted to be an official aid worker. Patrick listened intently, and realized just how passionate she was about the aid work. He wished he could feel as enthusiastic about something like that in his life.

The meal arrived and there was a comfortable silence as they ate together. The food was delicious, they both agreed. Patrick found himself telling her all about his trip to Ireland. He talked about Elena for the first time since her death. Afterwards he felt slightly unburdened. Helena listened patiently, and sympathized with his loss. He told her about his parents, and their hopes that he would become just like his father. Helena sympathized, and her comments, actually made him laugh. She found this amusing too, and they sat laughing together at the state of Patrick's rich presumptuous life.

Patrick paid the bill when they had finished, and they left arm in arm casually walking out to his car. He opened the car door for her, and she gracefully slid in revealing her thigh. He loosened his collar slightly as he felt suddenly a little too warm. He got in behind the wheel. "Thanks I really enjoyed the meal and your company of course." She added. He smiled, and turned on some soft music as the sleek car pulled away smoothly. They drove on comfortably, and listened to the provocative sounds of Lovers Rock while a million stars twinkled in the dark night sky.

When they reached her home Helena asked if he would like to come in for coffee. Patrick agreed eagerly, and followed her into the small terraced house. She lived alone apart from a little black kitten called Star. Patrick felt a little awkward as he had never been in such a small house. It seemed a little claustrophobic although he remained polite. He sat down on the worn settee. Helena left him for a moment as she went into the kitchen to make coffee. Patrick hoped that the cups were not chipped. She came back a few minutes later with perfect china mugs. When she sat beside him on the settee he felt a sudden urge to kiss her. The feeling was certainly mutual, but she fought to restrain her emotions, and thought this was not the moment to seduce him. After all it was only their first night out together what was she thinking!

Patrick reached for the coffee mug and sipped, but he couldn't keep his eyes off her slender legs. He suddenly remembered Elena, and how passionately they had made love. A sudden yearning grew between his thighs, and he slowly placed the coffee mug down onto the table. Helena gazed up into his mysterious blue eyes as a fiery passion exchanged between them. Patrick took hold of her, and pulled her towards him kissing her soft mouth, and feeling her body against his. At first she responded melting at his touch. His tender kiss was soft and warm, but he wanted so much more. His urgency startled her as she felt his hand slide up her thigh. "No!" Helena exclaimed and pulled away suddenly.

Patrick stopped immediately, and he was mortified that he'd got it so wrong. "I'm sorry." He said panting heavily. He couldn't disguise the tension in his body as he stood up. "I should go." He whispered and moved towards the door. Helena took a deep breath, her mind was flipping over in turmoil; physically she wanted him to stay, but some shred of morality held her tongue. Patrick apologized again and then left.

He sped off in his car feeling embarrassed and more than frustrated. When he arrived home to his luxury apartment he felt lonely and dejected. He tried to make sense of his feelings. After showering he lay in a black toweling robe, on his large empty bed. He closed his eyes, but couldn't sleep as thoughts whirled around in his head.

Patrick thought he heard a soft voice whisper close by, and he looked anxiously around the large luxurious bedroom. He sighed, and closed his eyes again, but just then he felt his cheek lightly brushed by a tender kiss. Patrick kept his eyes tightly closed; he knew he wouldn't see her, but he smiled and he was so glad that she had come. "I love you…Elena." He whispered into the dark night. The curtains moved ever so slightly, and her spirit stood watching over him as he drifted into sleep. "I'm here my love." Her spirit whispered. Patrick slept peacefully late into the next morning.

A week passed by since the incidental dinner date. Patrick had avoided the little Charity shop. He felt sure that Helena wouldn't want to see him. He had sent a large bouquet of flowers to the shop, and a small card of apology was attached. Then he kept himself busy, studying on his computer mainly. He visited the local library where he went just to find some company. Patrick avoided his parents as much as possible, but he did accept a dinner invitation from his mother. She was frantic to see him, and informed him that Lady Isabella Imogen Stubbs would be attending the dinner. She seemed perplexed by his sheer lack of enthusiasm.

A fortnight passed by, and Patrick decided that he would make an appearance at the Charity shop the next day. After a boring evening with his parents, and sour Lady Isabella Imogen he felt in need of Helena's exciting company. He had missed her, and hoped she could forgive him. A sudden thought came to Patrick; he went over to his parents' home immediately. Entering through the back door he went straight to the main kitchen, where cook was busily peeling vegetables. They greeted each other pleasantly. She watched Patrick curiously as he took several china cups and saucers from a cupboard.

"I need these over at the apartment." He said casually putting them into a cardboard box. Cook passed no remark, and she just continued with her task. He took the box out to his car, and loaded it straight into the boot. There were also a couple of other boxes, which he intended to donate to the shop too.

The next morning Patrick dressed hurriedly and straight after breakfast he headed off to town. When he entered the Charity shop, and heard the little bell tinkle overhead he smiled. Mary the older woman looked surprised to see him, but she helped him off load his boxes. They carried them together through to the back of the shop.

"Where's Helena? Is she out on her break?" Patrick asked suddenly noticing Mary's bewildered expression. Mary put the last box down, and went out to the glass counter. There she retrieved a white envelope, which she handed to Patrick. He didn't know what to think, but carefully opened it and found a hand written letter, which read:

Dear Patrick,

I'm so sorry for the way things happened, but I just wasn't sure of my feelings. The flowers were beautiful thank you. I accept your apology, and I hope we will always be friends. The most amazing opportunity -came up. There was a vacancy for a volunteer to work in Ethiopia. After an immediate interview, I was accepted for the post. It's the chance of a lifetime for me to do something so worthwhile, and so dear to my heart. I leave on Tuesday 16th on an evening flight. The post is for six months so I'll be away some time. Hopefully we will meet again in the future. Take care and have a happy life. Helena xxx

Patrick held the letter, and shook his head not quite believing what he had just read. A strange misted look came into his eyes. He thanked Mary, and walked out of the shop slightly dazed clutching the letter. Suddenly he felt his mobile phone vibrate. He reached for it, but saw there was no new message only Elena's last message bleeping. Patrick switched the phone off, and headed back to his car. He drove home in complete silence to his apartment.

On his arrival Patrick went inside, and immediately poured himself a brandy. He drank it straight back in one gulp, and then he poured another. His head swam as he was unused to the strong liquor. "Why is my life such a mess?" Patrick shouted loudly, and his voice taunted him with inertia. He slammed the empty glass down hard on the table. It shattered instantly, and sent shards of crystal flying through the air. "Damn!" He shouted again, and then jumped quite startled as his phone bleeped loudly. A message flashed, and he knew instinctively it was Elena's last message. Patrick stood quietly now, and he listened to her voice. When it had finished he slowly placed the phone down, and sat down at the table. For a long time he just sat there staring, at the silent phone. Not a sound could be heard above his slow steady breathing.

Patrick leapt up suddenly, and ran to his dressing room. He grabbed a hold-all, and began packing his clothes. He raced to his bedside cabinet, and retrieved his passport. He picked up his wallet, phone and car keys, and he left his apartment slamming the door on the way out. Patrick took a deep breath as he turned the ignition, and the car sprang into life. He patted the dashboard affectionately, grateful that the car had never faltered.

He drove off smoothly along the gravel drive, and passed by his parent's mansion, which was all lit up in the evening by fabulous chandeliers. He saw his father standing at the large drawing room window, no doubt taking his evening tipple. Patrick drove on quickly, glancing at his watch which showed eight thirty. Just as he got as far as the huge iron- gates, his mobile phone rang out. He brought the car to a halt sharply, and reached for his phone. It was his mother's number showing on the caller display. "Oh God mother, not now please!" Patrick sighed exasperated, but answered it hastily. "We were just wondering if you are alright dear." His mother asked. "And also where you might be going?" She added feebly.

Patrick laughed almost hysterically. "I'm fine mother; actually I'm just off to Africa!" He hung up, and decided not to delay any further as he sped off into the night.

It was just under an hour's drive to the airport. Patrick was not thinking rationally he knew, but he hoped this was the right airport. He prayed she would be there and not have already gone. He tried to rationalize things; planning how he would explain, but the words wouldn't come to him. Instead he turned on his stereo rather loudly, and concentrated on driving. Soon he was on the motorway, and headed in the direction of the airport. There was another airport of course as it was a city he lived in, but he continued to the nearest one.

At twenty past nine Patrick pulled into the airport slip road. A police car appeared behind him, and Patrick wondered for one insane second, whether his parents had sent the police to stop him leaving. The police car shadowed him, and Patrick began to feel a little nervous. Just then it pulled out and over took him, driving on ahead. Patrick sighed with relief, and drove on steadily to the airport car park. He turned into the long stay car park, and laughed at the irony.

The airport was brightly lit up, and bustling with activity. Patrick felt a little overwhelmed as he entered through the departure doors. He took a deep breath, and tried to instill confidence as he walked forward into the milling crowd. He headed towards an information desk, and his phone rang out loudly. Without glancing down he turned it off, he felt certain it was his mother again.

Patrick reached the information desk, and joined the short queue, he felt impatient so started tapping his foot on the hard floor. He huffed and sighed and tapped his foot until eventually his turn came. When he'd got the necessary details, he ran to the booking desk. Patrick pleaded with the man at the front of the queue, to let him jump in. The old man succumbed and let Patrick go ahead. "Thank you!" He felt as though his heart would burst with excitement as he asked for his flight ticket.

The ticket saleswoman shook her head in dismay. "The flights already boarded, and I think the gates have closed." She said apologetically.

"No! They can't have I need to be one that plane. The woman I intend to marry is on that flight!"

"Ah!" The people resounded in unison as they started nudging each other and whispering. Patrick stared into the sales woman's eyes as if she alone held the key to his future happiness; he held his breath as the seconds ticked by.

"Ah go on can't you stop the plane missus?" Someone in the queue shouted up. The saleswoman took a deep breath, and exhaled loudly. She sprang into action suddenly reaching for her desk phone.

"Okay I'll try." She looked at Patrick while she dialed.

"YES!" A shout resounded from the crowd. Patrick stood frozen with fear as he waited. His eyes fixed on her watching her expression.

"Shush!" She waved a commanding hand at the babbling queue. Then she spoke professionally into the phone, and a broad smile passed over her face as she replaced the receiver. She keyed in the ticket number as she spoke to Patrick. "You're in luck sir; the flight has been delayed by twenty minutes." She smiled as she handed him the ticket and checked his passport. She directed him to security check point.

"Thanks!" Patrick beamed, and leaned over the counter to kiss her cheek before running off with ticket, and boarding pass in hand.

Patrick placed his bag and other items on the conveyer belt. He walked straight through the electronic security entrance without it bleeping. He retrieved his items, and then he looked for gate sixty-seven. Patrick ran for all his life was worth, clutching his bag. He weaved his way through the mass of passengers, which were all going in opposite directions. He jumped the escalator stairs three at a time, and almost lost his balance as he collided with a woman at the bottom. "I'm sorry!" He shouted apologetically as he ran on frantically. He didn't bother with the walk on escalator, but sprinted alongside it instead.

 When he passed gate sixty- one his heart was pounding, and ready to burst from his chest. He'd got a stitch in his side, and was sweating profusely. Patrick stopped for just a second, and he could see gate sixty- seven, fifty yards ahead. He tried to catch his breath, and he almost feinted. A last surge of energy burst forth, and he was running ahead again feeling sick with excitement.

There was no one at gate sixty- seven, so Patrick just ran through into the tunnel gangway. His footsteps thudded heavily as he ran, and he couldn't stop himself. When he reached the open hatch of the plane's door he tripped, falling head over heels. He lay sprawled on the floor of the plane to the astonishment of the cabin crew.

"Have you got your boarding pass sir?" An air hostess helped him up.

"Yes." Patrick panted handing her the pass. He was shown to his seat, and he glanced hopefully at the many faces, which he passed walking up the aisle.

After an agonizing twenty minute wait while the plane took off, and reached its required altitude eventually the sign flashed to undo seat belts. Patrick sprang from his seat and began his search. He went the whole length of the plane looking at every person's face. When he got to the last row of seats his heart sank, Helena wasn't on the plane!

Oh my God! Patrick thought in alarm. He hadn't made provision in his plans for this, and he had taken it for granted that she would be on the plane. After all he had been through to get this far, it just wouldn't sink in. The thought of returning home without her, filled him with a sudden dread.

He turned around to return to his seat, when all of a sudden there she was! Helena! She was rushing up the aisle towards him. "Patrick what on earth are you doing here?" She asked in astonishment. It was one of those fleeting moments when your body reacts, and then your brain catches up later. It's when you see someone who you recognize, but you still automatically ask if it's them.

"Helena!" Patrick ran forward, and threw his arms around her burying his face in her shoulder. He gasped almost on the verge of tears because he thought he had lost her. He took her face in his hands, and kissed her passionately releasing his over wrought emotions. She responded, and the kiss lingered on regardless of the onlookers.

The airbus continued flying on through the night, and into the morning. High above the clouds entwined in each other's arms, they flew on to the other side of the world.

Chapter Thirteen

Six months later Patrick and Helena had returned to England, and they were engaged. They had worked side by side in the desolate Ethiopian aid camp. Patrick's medical school training had been extremely useful, and he had worked tirelessly in the makeshift hospital tent. He had worked alongside accomplished humanitarian doctors, which had come together from the four corners of the earth. Helena had enjoyed helping the mothers, and young babies supplying food to them at the makeshift kitchen.

At night they had lain in each other's arms beneath the stars, with only a tent for shelter. The days were long and the heat was unbearable at times. They had suffered sunburn, insect bites, and occasional diarrhea due to the rough conditions of the camp. Neither one had complained because they were happy just to be there with each other. They knew they were helping those truly in need.

When they were back in England Helena persuaded Patrick to return to medical school. They planned to return to Africa once he became qualified. There were many vacant posts, and surgeons were always needed.

Patrick and Helena had planned to marry at Christmas much to the delight of his parents. They had finally realized during Patrick's long absence just how precious he was to them. Patrick's mother had instilled into her husband the importance of their son's happiness. It was imperative if their estate were to be maintained. They didn't want to lose contact, or become estranged with their only son and heir. Patrick's parents had changed their pious attitudes dramatically, and welcomed his fiancée. His mother was ecstatic and secretly hoped for many grandchildren from their union.

There were only a few weeks left of British summertime. Those long warm, hazy days would be soon be replaced by the cooler damp autumn. Patrick would soon be back at medical school, and he and Helena would be entrenched with their wedding arrangements. So just for now he decided to savor the last of the long summer days, and was determined to enjoy the peaceful lull in his new life.

Helena had broken the idyllic peace. She planned to go to Ireland for a long weekend to visit her sister, who had just had a baby. She was really excited to be an Aunty at long last. Patrick reluctantly agreed to go with her after much coaxing and cajoling. So here they were boarding yet another plane, for the short flight to Ireland. The flight took less than an hour, and was forty five minutes to be precise. They arrived in Dublin, Ireland's capital city, where they then hired a car at the airport.

Patrick was unusually quiet as they drove out of the city. They took the western route, and headed on the M4 out towards Athlone. Helena chatted excitedly non-stop about her sister; she wondered who the baby took after in looks. Patrick remained silent, and he shrugged his shoulders to her constant queries. A couple of hours later they had passed Athlone, and were in the county of Galway. Patrick followed the coastal road to Bell harbour, where Helena's sister lived. The sea breeze wafted in through the open car window, and Patrick's mind recalled a similar journey as his senses relived the past. The scenery was outstanding, and a far cry from the hot desert plains of Africa.

They had arrived at the bungalow, which was aptly named Sea view. Helena's sister and her husband Padraig were there to greet them. The next few hours were spent leisurely chatting while drinking tea, and eating sandwiches and cakes. The endless chatter between the sisters involved babies, weddings, christenings and so on. Padraig had escaped after the first hour as he had farm work to see to. The women didn't seem to mind his absence and carried on regardless.

Patrick was only sort of half listening, and he remarked politely in agreement to whatever was being said. He glanced over to the open window as a sudden gust of sea breeze rustled the curtains. He breathed in deeply, relishing its freshness. Just then he had a sudden thought. He stood up, and waited for a slight pause in the conversation. "I think I'll just go for a drive, and leave you two alone to chat."

Helena noticed his strange expression, but decided against questioning him. "Okay love."
He kissed her lightly on the cheek before leaving. Patrick checked the map before starting the engine, and then he drove off steadily.

It was dusk when he arrived at White Rose Cottage. He parked the car beside the stone wall with the rusty iron- gate. The heady scent of damask roses filled the air. Patrick breathed in their magical scent. He pushed the open the rusty gate, and the memories came flooding back. He didn't go into the cottage, but decided instead to go around to the back garden. There was the old deck chair still positioned on the lawn, where he had sat in it that summer. Beyond the lawn he saw the white picket fence, and the small wooden gate which led to the beach. There was just a moment's hesitation, and then he ran towards it eagerly. Patrick stopped dead in his tracks as the spectacular view rendered him speechless. Just as it had the very first time he saw it. The words fell from his mouth. "Wow it's still as beautiful."

He descended the sandy track, which led down to the golden sands and the beach below. The shimmering blue sea mesmerized his senses. The breeze stirred up the sand in whirling little gusts. Patrick removed his shoes and socks, and unbuttoned his shirt. He gasped with sheer delight as he felt the cool air caress his bare skin. It was exhilarating just like the first time. He walked to the edge of the shore, and stood still just gazing out at the slow moving waves, which heaved to and fro.

The sun began to sink on the distant horizon, and cool waves rippled over his bare feet. Patrick stood unmoved as if frozen in time. His gaze lingered on the restless water and the distant horizon. His mind wandered back to that particular summer day, when he had first seen Elena as she emerged from the sea. In his mind he saw her as she walked towards him. She wore her skimpy white bikini, and droplets of water shimmered like gold on her tanned curvaceous body. "She was so beautiful!" Patrick spoke softly, and he sighed heavily shaking his head in disbelief.

He began to walk along the deserted beach towards the secret cove where they had made love. He passed around the headland, and a chill breeze blew through his hair. Patrick splashed clumsily through a slimy rock pool, and soaked the legs of his rolled up trousers. Just then as he came to the entrance of the hideaway cave he couldn't go in. The memories became too vivid and so very painful. Patrick sank down to his knees, buried his face in his hands and cried.

He cried because he loved her intensely, and she was his first true love. He missed her so much, and his body ached for her. Patrick felt sure his heart was breaking all over again at that very moment in time. Enormous loud wailing sobs wracked his body, and he felt lost and so very alone. He'd lost the love of his life, and he felt his will to live ebbing away with the tide. At that moment he suddenly had doubts about Helena, and doubts about their forthcoming wedding. How on earth could he possibly ever love another, without feeling somehow that he was betraying Elena? He would end up sad and alone, but always loving Elena he lamented. These were the melancholic thoughts, which were suddenly flooding his tortured mind.

The pale moon rose against the dark night sky, and a cool breeze drifted towards Patrick as he lay huddled up on the beach. The wind skipped, and danced through the cave just like a playful spirit. It blew around Patrick, and stirred him with a light gentle kiss on his mouth. He heard his name called out carried on the whisper of the soft sea breeze. "Patrick." Elena called out to him.

"Elena." Patrick called out to her as he got up slowly. He felt certain she was there although he couldn't see her. He felt dazed and emotionally drained as he started to walk along the sand. In his mind he sensed she had come as she had before, when he had felt so utterly desolate.

Patrick started to walk along the beach, and he wondered if maybe she knew what he was thinking. Maybe she sensed that he was having doubts about the forthcoming wedding. If only she could talk to him, and tell him what he should do. His mind started wandering again, he felt so very confused. The memories rolled in ceaselessly like the tide. Just then Patrick had a flashback, and he remembered the last time he had seen Elena. It had been through the pub window, and she had been with those other men!

The sea grew restless out in the bay and Patrick's mood changed. He became angry as the jealousy he'd felt that day returned to haunt him with a vengeance. "Maybe you didn't really love me Elena?" He shouted loudly, wildly into the sea breeze. The waves grew stronger and they rushed head long towards the shore. Dark clouds scudded across the sky momentarily obscuring the full moon. The cove was shrouded in a heavy black melancholic shadow.

Patrick shivered as he continued to walk, carefully picking his way around the large craggy rocks. He sighed heavily, and then spoke aloud. "I'm sorry Elena; I think I really came here just to say thank you and goodbye." He said sadly. "You brought me to life, and taught me how to love, and I will always love you." Tears rolled down Patrick's cheeks, and he tried to speak clearly. "I guess what I really wanted was a sign. Can you just give me something to let me know you forgive me?" He spluttered, and his words got caught up on the high westerly winds. I can't go on anymore, there's just no point to anything. He shuddered as he felt emotionally wrecked and exhausted.

Patrick turned away from the tumultuous sea, and he started to walk back towards White Rose Cottage. Suddenly he heard his name shouted loudly, it was unmistakable...... "Patrick!"....He turned around, and then he saw her....Elena in ghostly form wearing her white bikini.

Patrick stood rooted to the spot, and not daring to move. "Oh my God!" His heart thudded in his chest. She came towards him, and he felt sure he must have died and this was heaven. He couldn't believe he could actually see her. She smiled, and her beautiful smile melted his heart just like it had the first time they met. Tears streamed from Patrick's eyes, rolling down his face. Elena reached out her hand, and gently wiped them away. "No more tears my love." She whispered softly.

He reached out to her, and pulled her towards him as he wrapped his arms around her in a tight embrace. The dark clouds parted revealing a bright silver full moon, which shone down on the lovers entwined silhouette. The hands of time stood completely still, allowing the star-crossed lovers just one last kiss.

Elena released herself from Patrick's embrace. "I have to go my love." She whispered softly. He stood still as his eyes pleaded with her not to leave him, but in his heart he knew she couldn't stay. Patrick heaved a deep heart wrenching sigh, and he watched Elena walk towards the sea. The swelling waves rushed forward and immersed her completely. She disappeared beneath the deep blue waters of the ocean. All that remained was a heart, which was drawn in the wet sand, and there at its center she had written their names Elena & *Patrick*....

Printed in Great Britain
by Amazon